RIDING FOR
THE BRAND

**Center Point
Large Print**

Also by Louis L'Amour and available from Center Point Large Print:

Trailing West
Big Medicine
Hanging Woman Creek
West of the Tularosa
Flint
The Man from Battle Flat
Borden Chantry
The High Graders

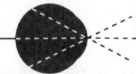

This Large Print Book carries the Seal of Approval of N.A.V.H.

RIDING FOR THE BRAND

A WESTERN TRIO

LOUIS L'AMOUR

CENTER POINT PUBLISHING
THORNDIKE, MAINE

This Circle Ⓥ Western is published by
Center Point Large Print in 2011 in co-operation with
Golden West Literary Agency.

Copyright © 2011 by Golden West Literary Agency.

First Edition, March 2011.

The text of this Large Print edition is unabridged.
In other aspects, this book may vary
from the original edition.
Printed in the United States of America
on permanent paper.
Set in 16-point Times New Roman type.

ISBN: 978-1-60285-991-3

Library of Congress Cataloging-in-Publication Data

L'Amour, Louis, 1908-1988.
  Riding for the brand : a western trio / Louis L'Amour ; edited by Jon Tuska. — 1st ed.
  p. cm.
  ISBN 978-1-60285-991-3 (library binding : alk. paper)
  1. Large type books. I. Tuska, Jon. II. Title.
PS3523.A446R55 2011
813′.52—dc22
                                                          2010041692

TABLE OF CONTENTS

Foreword
by Jon Tuska

Louis Dearborn LaMoore (1908-1988) was born in
Jamestown, North Dakota. He left home at fifteen
and subsequently held a wide variety of jobs
although he worked mostly as a merchant seaman.
From his earliest youth, L'Amour had a love of
verse. His first published work was a poem, "The
Chap Worth While", appearing when he was
eighteen years old in his former hometown's
newspaper, the *Jamestown Sun*. It is the only poem
from his early years that he left out of *Smoke from
This Altar* which appeared in 1939 from Lusk
Publishers in Oklahoma City, a book which
L'Amour published himself; however, this poem is
reproduced in *The Louis L'Amour Companion*
(Andrews and McMeel, 1992) edited by Robert
Weinberg. L'Amour wrote poems and articles for a
number of small circulation arts magazines all
through the early 1930s and, after hundreds of
rejection slips, finally had his first story accepted,
"Anything for a Pal" in *True Gang Life* (10/35). He
returned in 1938 to live with his family where they
had settled in Choctaw, Oklahoma, determined to
make writing his career. He wrote a fight story
bought by Standard Magazines that year and
became acquainted with editor Leo Margulies who
was to play an important rôle later in L'Amour's

life. "The Town No Guns Could Tame" in *New Western* (3/40) was his first published Western story.

During the Second World War L'Amour was drafted and ultimately served with the U.S. Army Transportation Corps in Europe. However, in the two years before he was shipped out, he managed to write a great many adventure stories for Standard Magazines. The first story he published in 1946, the year of his discharge, was a Western, "Law of the Desert Born" in *Dime Western* (4/46). A talk with Leo Margulies resulted in L'Amour's agreeing to write Western stories for the various Western pulp magazines published by Standard Magazines, a third of which appeared under the byline Jim Mayo, the name of a character in L'Amour's earlier adventure fiction. The proposal for L'Amour to write new Hopalong Cassidy novels came from Margulies who wanted to launch *Hopalong Cassidy's Western Magazine* to take advantage of the popularity William Boyd's old films and new television series were enjoying with a new generation. Doubleday & Company agreed to publish the pulp novelettes in hard cover books. L'Amour was paid $500 a story, no royalties, and he was assigned the house name Tex Burns. L'Amour read Clarence E. Mulford's books about the Bar-20 and based his Hopalong Cassidy on Mulford's original creation. Only two issues of the magazine appeared before it ceased publication.

Doubleday felt that the Hopalong character had to appear exactly as William Boyd did in the films and on television and thus the four novels L'Amour wrote had to be revamped to meet with this requirement prior to publication in book form.

L'Amour's first Western novel under his own byline was *Westward the Tide* (World's Work, 1950). It was rejected by every American publisher to which it was submitted. World's Work paid a flat £75 without royalties for British Empire rights in perpetuity. L'Amour sold his first Western short story to a slick magazine a year later, "The Gift of Cochise" in *Collier's* (7/5/52). Robert Fellows and John Wayne purchased screen rights to this story from L'Amour for $4,000 and James Edward Grant, one of Wayne's favorite screenwriters, developed a script from it, changing L'Amour's Ches Lane to Hondo Lane. L'Amour retained the right to novelize Grant's screenplay, which differs substantially from his short story, and he was able to get an endorsement from Wayne to be used as a blurb, stating that *Hondo* was the finest Western Wayne had ever read. *Hondo* (Fawcett Gold Medal, 1953) by Louis L'Amour was released on the same day as the film, *Hondo* (Warner, 1953), with a first printing of 320,000 copies.

With *Showdown at Yellow Butte* (Ace, 1953) by Jim Mayo, L'Amour began a series of short Western novels for Don Wollheim that could be doubled with other short novels by other authors in

Ace Publishing's paperback two-fers. Advances on these were $800 and usually the author never earned any royalties. *Heller with a Gun* (Fawcett Gold Medal, 1955) was the first of a series of original Westerns L'Amour had agreed to write under his own name following the success for Fawcett of *Hondo*. L'Amour wanted even this early to have his Western novels published in hard cover editions. He expanded "Guns of the Timberland" by Jim Mayo in *West* (9/50) for *Guns of the Timberlands* (Jason Press, 1955), a hard cover Western for which he was paid an advance of $250. Another novel for Jason Press followed and then *Silver Cañon* (Avalon Books, 1956) for Thomas Bouregy & Company.

The great turn in L'Amour's fortunes came about because of problems Saul David was having with his original paperback Westerns program at Bantam Books. Fred Glidden had been signed to a contract to produce two original paperback Luke Short Western novels a year for an advance of $15,000 each. It was a long-term contract but, in the first ten years of it, Fred only wrote six novels. Literary agent Marguerite Harper then persuaded Bantam that Fred's brother, Jon, could help fulfill the contract and Jon was signed for eight Peter Dawson Western novels. When Jon died suddenly before completing even one book for Bantam, Harper managed to engage a ghost writer at the Disney studios to write these eight "Peter

Dawson" novels, beginning with *The Savages* (Bantam, 1959). They proved inferior to anything Jon had ever written and what sales they had seemed to be due only to the Peter Dawson name.

Saul David wanted to know from L'Amour if *he* could deliver two Western novels a year. L'Amour said he could, and he did. In fact, by 1962 this number was increased to three original paperback novels a year. The first L'Amour novel to appear under the Bantam contract was *Radigan* (Bantam, 1958).

Yet I feel that some of Louis L'Amour's finest work is to be found in his early magazine fiction. Several of those stories are collected here, reprinted as they first appeared, and possessing the characteristics in purest form that I suspect account in largest measure for the loyal following Louis L'Amour won from his readers: the young male hero who is in the process of growing into manhood and who is evaluating other human beings and his own experiences; a resourceful frontier woman who has beauty as well as fortitude; and the powerful, romantic, strangely compelling vision of the American West that invests L'Amour's Western fiction and makes it such a delightful escape from the cares of a later time—in this author's words, that "big country needing big men and women to live in it" and where there was no place for "the frightened or the mean."

RIDING FOR THE BRAND

A WESTERN TRIO

The Lion Hunter and the Lady

The mountain lion stared down at him with wild, implacable eyes and snarled deep in its chest. He was big, one of the biggest Morgan had seen in his four years of hunting them. The lion crouched on a thick limb not over eight feet above his head.

"Watch him, Cat," Lone John Williams warned. "He's the biggest I ever seen. The biggest in these mountains, I'll bet."

"You ever seen Lop-Ear?" Morgan queried, watching the lion. "He's half again bigger than this one." He jumped as he spoke, caught a limb in his left hand, and then swung himself up as easily as a trapeze performer.

The lion came to its feet then and crouched, growling wickedly, threatening the climbing man. But Morgan continued to mount toward the lion.

"Give me that pole!" Morgan called to the older man. "I'll have this baby in another minute!"

"You watch it," Williams warned. "That lion ain't foolin'."

Never in the year he had been working with Cat Morgan had Lone John become accustomed to seeing a man go up a tree after a mountain lion. Yet in that period Morgan had captured more than fifty lions alive and had killed as many more. Morgan was not a big man as big men are counted, but he was tall, lithe, and extraordinarily strong. Agile as a cat, he climbed trees, cliffs, and rocky slopes after the big cats, for which he was named, and had made a good thing out of supplying zoo and circus animal buyers.

With a noose at the end of the pole, and only seven feet below the snarling beast, Morgan lifted the pole with great care. The lion struck viciously and then struck again, and in that instant after the second strike, Morgan put the loop around his neck and drew the noose tight. Instantly the cat became a snarling, clawing, spitting fury, but Morgan swung down from the tree, dragging the beast after him.

Before the yapping dogs could close with him, Lone John tossed his own loop, snaring the lion's hind legs. Morgan closed with the animal, got a loop around the powerful forelegs, and drew it tight. In a matter of seconds the mountain lion was neatly trussed and muzzled, with a stick thrust into its jaws between its teeth, and its jaws tied shut with rawhide.

Morgan drew a heavy sack around the animal and then tied it at the neck, leaving the lion's head outside.

Straightening, Cat Morgan took out the makings and began to roll a smoke. "Well," he said, as he put the cigarette between his lips, "that's one more and one less."

Hard-ridden horses sounded in the woods and then a half dozen riders burst from the woods and a yell rent the air. "Got 'em, Dave! Don't move, you!" The guns the men held backed up their argument, and Cat Morgan relaxed slowly, his eyes straying from one face to another, finally settling on the big man who rode last from out of the trees.

This man was not tall, but blocky and powerful. His neck was thick and his jaw wide. He was clean-shaven, unusual in this land of beards and mustaches. His face wore a smile of unconcealed satisfaction now, and, swinging down, he strode toward them. "So, you finally got caught, didn't you? Now how smart do you feel?"

"Who do you think we are?" Morgan asked coolly. "I never saw you before."

"I reckon not, but we trailed you right here. You've stole your last horse. Shake out a loop, boys. We'll string 'em up right here."

"Be careful with that talk," Lone John said. "We ain't horse thieves an' ain't been out of the hills in more'n a year. You've got the wrong men."

"That's tough," the big man said harshly, "because you hang, here and now."

"Maybe they ain't the men, Dorfman. After all, we lost the trail back yonder a couple of miles." The speaker was a slender man with black eyes and swarthy face.

Without turning, Dorfman said sharply: "Shut up! When I want advice from a 'breed, I'll ask it."

His hard eyes spotted the burlap sack. The back

17

of it lay toward him, and the lion's head was faced away from him. All he saw was the lump of the filled sack. "What's this? Grub?" He kicked hard at the sack, and from it came a snarl of fury.

Dorfman jumped and staggered back, his face white with shock. Somebody laughed, and Dorfman wheeled, glaring around for the offender. An old man with gray hair and a keen, hard face looked at Morgan. "What's in that sack?" he demanded.

"A mountain lion," Cat replied calmly. "A nice, big, live lion. Make a good pet for your loud-mouthed friend." He paused and then smiled tolerantly at Dorfman. "If he wouldn't be scared of him."

Dorfman's face was livid. Furious that he had been frightened before these men, and enraged at Morgan as the cause of it, he sprang at Morgan and swung back a huge fist. Instantly Cat Morgan stepped inside the punch, catching it on an upraised forearm. At the same instant he whipped a wicked right uppercut to Dorfman's wind. The big man gasped and paled. He looked up, and Morgan stepped in and hooked hard to the body, and then the chin. Dorfman hit the ground in a lump.

Showing no sign of exertion, Morgan stepped back. He looked at the older man. "He asked for it," he said calmly. "I didn't mind, though." He glanced at Dorfman, who was regaining his breath and his senses, and then his eyes swung back to the older man. "I'm Cat Morgan, a lion hunter. This is Lone John Williams, my partner. What Lone John said was true. We haven't been out of the hills in a year."

"He's telling the truth." It was the half-breed. The man was standing beside the tree. "His hounds are tied right back here, an' from the look of this tree they just caught that cat. The wood is still wet where the bark was skimmed from the tree by his boots."

"All right, Loop." The older man's eyes came back to Morgan. "Sorry. Reckon we went off half-cocked. I've heard of you."

A wiry, yellow-haired cowhand leaned on his pommel. "You go up a tree for the cats?" he asked incredulously. "I wouldn't do it for a thousand dollars!"

Dorfman was on his feet. His lips were split and there was a cut on his cheek bone. One eye was rapidly swelling. He glared at Morgan. "I'll kill you for this!" he snarled.

Morgan looked at him. "I reckon you'll try," he said. "There ain't much man in you, just brute and beef."

The older man spoke up quickly. "Let's go, Dorf. This ain't catchin' our thief."

As the cavalcade straggled from the clearing, the man called Loop loitered behind. "Watch yourself, Morgan," he said quietly. "He's bad, that Dorfman.

He'll never rest until he kills you, now. He won't take it lyin' down."

"Thanks." Cat's gray-green eyes studied the half-breed. "What was stolen?"

Loop jerked his head. "Some of Dorfman's horses. Blooded stock, stallion, three mares, and four colts."

Morgan watched him go, and then walked back down the trail for the pack animals. When they had the cat loaded, Lone John left him to take it back to camp.

Mounting his own zebra dun, Morgan now headed downcountry to prospect a new cañon for cat sign. He had promised a dealer six lions and he had four of them. With luck he could get the other two this week. Only one of the hounds was with him, a big, ugly brute that was one of the two best lion dogs he had, just a mongrel. Big Jeb was shrewd beyond average. He weighed one hundred and twenty pounds and was tawny as the lions he chased.

The plateau was pine-clad, a thick growth that spilled over into the deep cañon beyond, and that cañon was a wicked jumble of wrecked ledges and broken rock. At the bottom he could hear the roar and tumble of a plunging mountain stream, although he had never seen it. That cañon should be home for a lot of lions.

There was no trail. The three of them—man, dog, and horse—sought a trail down, working their way along the rim over a thick cover of pine needles. At last Cat Morgan saw the slope fall away steeply, but at such a grade that he could walk the horse to the bottom. Slipping occasionally on the needles, they headed down.

Twice Jeb started to whine as he picked up old lion smell, but each time he was dissuaded by Cat's sharp-spoken command.

There was plenty of sign. In such a cañon as this it should take him no time at all to get his cats. He was walking his horse and rolling a smoke when he heard the sound of an axe. It brought him up, standing.

It was impossible! There could be nobody in this wild area, nobody! Not in all the days they had worked the region had they seen more than one or two men until they encountered the horse-thief hunters.

Carefully he went on, calling Jeb close to the horse and moving on with infinite care. Whoever was in this wilderness would be somebody he would want to see before he was seen. He remembered the horse thieves whose trail had been lost. Who else could it be?

Instantly he saw evidence of the correctness of his guess. In the dust at the mouth of the cañon were tracks of a small herd of horses.

Grimly he eased his Colt in the holster. Horse thieves were a common enemy, and, although he had no liking for Dorfman, this was his job, too.

Taller than most, Cat Morgan was slender of waist. Today he wore boots, but usually moccasins. His red flannel shirt was sun-faded and patched, his black jeans were saddle polished, and his face was brown from sun and wind, hollow-cheeked under the keen gray-green eyes. His old hat was black and flat-crowned. It showed rough usage.

Certainly the thief had chosen well. Nobody would ever find him back in here. The horses had turned off to the right. Following, Cat went down, through more tumbled rock and boulders, and then drew up on the edge of a clearing.

It was after sundown here. The shadows were long, but near the far wall was the black oblong of a cabin, and light streamed through a window and the wide-open door.

Dishes rattled, the sound of a spoon scraping something from a dish, and he heard a voice singing. A woman's voice.

Amazed, he started walking his horse nearer, yet the horse had taken no more than a step when he heard a shrill scream, a cry odd and inhuman, a cry that brought him up short. At the same instant, the light in the house went out and all was silent. Softly he spoke to his horse and walked on toward the house.

He heard the click of a back-drawn hammer, and a cool girl's voice said: "Stand right where you are, mister! And if you want to get a bullet through your belt buckle, just start something!"

"I'm not moving," Morgan said impatiently. "But this isn't a nice way to greet visitors."

"Who invited you?" she retorted. "What do you want, anyway? Who are you?"

"Cat Morgan. I'm a lion hunter. As for being invited, I've been a lot of places without being invited. Let me talk to your dad or your husband."

"You'll talk to me. Lead your horse and start walking straight ahead. My eyes are mighty good, so if you want to get shot, just try me."

With extreme care, Morgan walked on toward the house. When he was within a dozen paces, a shrill but harsh voice cried: "Stand where you are! Drop your guns!"

Impatiently Morgan replied: "I'll stand where I am, but I won't drop my guns. Light up and let's see who you are."

Someone moved, and later there was a light. Then the girl spoke. "Come in, you."

She held a double-barreled shotgun and she was well back inside the door. A tall, slender but well-shaped girl, she had rusty-red hair and a few scattered freckles. She wore a buckskin shirt that failed to conceal the lines of her lovely figure.

Her inspection of him was cool, careful. Then she looked at the big dog that had come in and stood alongside him. "Lion hunter? You the one who has that pack of hounds I hear nearby every day?"

He nodded. "I've been running lions up on the plateau. Catching 'em, too."

She stared. "Catching them? Alive? Sounds to me like you have more nerve than sense. What do you want live lions for?"

"Sell 'em to some circus or zoo. They bring anywhere from three to seven hundred dollars, depending on size and sex. That beats punching cows."

She nodded. "It sure does, but I reckon punching cows is a lot safer."

"How about you?" he said. "What's a girl doing up in a place like this? I didn't have any idea there was anybody back in here."

"Nor has anybody else up to now. You won't tell, will you? If you go out of here and tell, I'll be in trouble. Dorfman would be down here after me in a minute."

"For stealing horses?" Morgan asked shrewdly.

Her eyes flashed. "They are not his horses. They are mine. Every last one of them." She lowered the gun a trifle. "Dorfman is both a bully and a thief. He stole my dad's ranch, then his horses. That stallion is mine, and so are the mares and their get."

"Tell me about it," he suggested. Carefully he removed his hat.

She studied him doubtfully, and then lowered the gun. "I was just putting supper on. Draw up a chair."

"Let's eat!" a sharp voice yelled. Startled, Cat looked around and for the first time saw the parrot in the cage.

"That's Pancho," she explained. "He's a lot of company. I'm Laurie Madison."

Her father had been a trader among the Nez Percé Indians, and from them he obtained the splendid Appaloosa stallion and the mares from which his herd was started. When Karl Dorfman appeared, there had been trouble. Later, while she was East on a trip, her father had been killed by a fall from a horse. Returning, she found the ranch sold and the horses gone.

"They told me the stallion had thrown him. I knew better. It had been Dorfman and his partner, Ad Vetter, who found Dad. And then they brought bills against the estate and forced a quick sale of all property to satisfy them. The judge worked with them. Shortly after, the judge left and bought a ranch of his own. Dad never owed money to anyone. I believe they murdered him."

"That would be hard to prove. Did you have any evidence?"

"Only what the doctor said. He told me the blows could not have been made by the fall. He believed Dad had been struck while lying on the ground."

Cat Morgan believed her. Whether his own dislike of Dorfman influenced it, he did not know. Somehow the story rang true. He studied the

25

problem thoughtfully. "Did you get anything from the ranch?"

"Five hundred dollars and a ticket back East." Anger flashed in her eyes as she leaned toward him to refill his cup. "Mister Morgan, that ranch was worth at least forty thousand dollars. Dad had been offered that much and refused it."

"So you followed them?"

"Yes. I appeared to accept the situation, but discovered where Dorfman had gone and followed him, determined to get the horses back, at least."

It was easier, he discovered two hours later, to ride to the secret valley than to escape from it. After several false starts, he succeeded in finding the spot where the lion had been captured that day, and then hit the trail for camp. As he rode, the memory of Dorfman kept returning—a brutal, hard man, accustomed to doing as he chose. He had not seen the last of him, he knew.

Coming into the trees near the camp, Cat Morgan grew increasingly worried, for he smelled no smoke and saw no fire. Speaking to the horse, he rode into the basin and drew up sharply. Before him, suspended from a tree, was a long black burden!

Clapping the spurs to the horse, he crossed the clearing and grabbed the hanging figure. Grabbing his hunting knife, he slashed the rope that hung him from the tree, and then lowered the old man to the ground. Loosening his clothes, he held his hand over the old man's heart. Lone John was alive!

Swiftly Morgan built a fire and got water. The old man had not only been hanged, but had been shot twice through the body and once through the hand. But he was still alive.

The old man's lids fluttered, and he whispered: "Dorfman. Five of 'em. Hung me . . . heard somethin' . . . they done . . . took off." He breathed hoarsely for a bit. "Figured it . . . it was you . . . reckon."

"*Shhh*. Take it easy now, John. You'll be all right."

"No. I'm done for. That rope . . . I grabbed it . . . held my weight till I plumb give out."

The wiry old hand gripping his own suddenly eased its grip, and the old man was dead.

Grimly Cat got to his feet. Carefully he packed what gear had not been destroyed. The cats had been tied off a few yards from the camp and had not been found. He scattered meat to them, put water within their reach, and returned to his horse. A moment only, he hesitated. His eyes wide open to what lay ahead, he lifted the old man across the saddle of a horse, and then mounted his own. The trail he took led to Seven Pines.

It was the gray hour before the dawn when he rode into the town. Up the street was the sheriff's office. He knocked a long time before there was a reply. Then a hard-faced man with blue and cold eyes opened the door. "What's the matter? What's up?"

"My partner's been murdered. Shot down, then hung."

"Hung?" The sheriff stared at him, no friendly light in his eyes. "Who hung him?"

"Dorfman. There were five in the outfit."

The sheriff's face altered perceptibly at the name. He walked out and untied the old man's body, lowering it to the stoop before the office. He scowled. "I reckon," he said dryly, "if Dorfman done it, he had good reason. You better light out if you want to stay in one piece."

Unbelieving, Morgan stared at him. "You're the sheriff?" he demanded. "I'm charging Dorfman with murder. I want him arrested."

"You want?" The sheriff glared. "Who the devil are you? If Dorfman hung this man, he had good reason. He's lost horses. I reckon he figured this *hombre* was one of the thieves. Now you slope it afore I lock you up."

Cat Morgan drew back three steps, his eyes on the sheriff. "I see. Lock me up, eh? Sheriff, you'd have a mighty hard job locking me up. What did you say your name was?"

"Vetter, if it makes any difference."

"Vetter, eh? Ad Vetter?" Morgan was watching the sheriff like a cat.

Sheriff Vetter looked at him sharply. "Yes, Ad Vetter. What about it?"

28

Cat Morgan took another step back toward his horses, his eyes cold now. "Ad Vetter . . . a familiar name in the Nez Percé country."

Vetter started as if struck. "What do you mean by that?"

Morgan smiled. "Don't you know," he said, chancing a long shot, "that you and Dorfman are wanted up there for murdering old man Madison?"

"You're a liar!" Sheriff Vetter's face was white as death. He drew back suddenly, and Morgan could almost see the thought in the man's mind and knew that his accusation had marked him for death. "If Dorfman finds you here, he'll hang you, too."

Cat Morgan backed away slowly, watching Vetter. The town was coming awake now, and he wracked his brain for a solution to the problem. Obviously Dorfman was a man with influence here, and Ad Vetter was sheriff. Whatever Morgan did or claimed was sure to put him in the wrong. And then he remembered the half-breed, Loop, and the older man who had cautioned Dorfman the previous afternoon.

A man was sweeping the steps before the saloon, and Morgan stopped beside him. "Know a man named Loop? A 'breed?"

"Sure do." The sweeper straightened and measured Morgan. "Huntin' him?"

"Yeah, and another *hombre*. Older feller, gray hair, pleasant face but frosty eyes. The kind that

29

could be mighty bad if pushed too hard. I think I heard him called Dave."

"That'll be Allen. Dave Allen. He owns the D over A, west of town. Loop lives right on the edge of town in a shack. He can show you where Dave lives."

Turning abruptly, Morgan swung into the saddle and started out of town. As he rounded the curve toward the bridge, he glanced back. Sheriff Vetter was talking to the sweeper. Cat reflected grimly that it would do him but little good, for unless he had talked with Dorfman the previous night, and he did not seem to have, he would not understand Morgan's reason for visiting the old rancher. And Cat knew that he might be wasting his time.

He recognized Loop's shack by the horse in the corral and drew up before it. The half-breed appeared in the door, wiping an ear with a towel. He was surprised when he saw Cat Morgan, but he listened as Morgan told him quickly about the hanging of Lone John Williams and Vetter's remarks.

"No need to ride after Allen," Loop said. "He's comin' down the road now. Him and Tex Norris. They was due in town this mornin'."

At Loop's hail, the two riders turned abruptly toward the cabin. Dave Allen listened in silence while Cat repeated his story, only now he told all, not that he had seen the girl or knew where she was, but that he had learned why the horses were stolen, and then about the strange death of old man Madison. Dave Allen sat his horse in silence and listened. Tex spat once, but made no other comment until the end. "That's Dorfman, boss. I never did cotton to him."

"Wait." Allen's eyes rested thoughtfully on Cat. "Why tell me? What do you want me to do?"

Cat Morgan smiled suddenly, and, when Tex saw that smile, he found himself pleased that it was Dorfman this man wanted and not him. "Why, Allen, I don't want you to do anything. Only, I'm not an outlaw. I don't aim to become one for a no-account like Dorfman, nor another like this here Vetter. You're a big man hereabouts, so I figured to tell you my story and let you see my side of this before the trouble starts."

"You aim to go after him?"

Morgan shook his head. "I'm a stranger here, Allen. He's named me for a horse thief, and the law's against me, too. I aim to let them come to me, right in the middle of town."

Loop walked back into his cabin, and, when he came out, he had a Spencer .56, and, mounting, he fell in beside Morgan. "You'll get a fair break," he said quietly, his eyes cold and steady. "I aim to see it. No man who wasn't all right would come out like that and state his case. Besides, you know that old man Williams struck me like a mighty fine old gent."

Dorfman was standing on the steps as they rode up. One eye was barely open, the other swollen. The marks of the beating were upon him. That he had been talking to Vetter was obvious by his manner, although the sheriff was nowhere in sight. Several hardcase cowhands loitered about, the presence creating no puzzle to Cat Morgan.

Karl Dorfman glared at Allen. "You're keepin' strange company, Dave."

The old man's eyes chilled. "You aimin' to tell me who I should travel with, Dorfman? If you are, save your breath. We're goin' to settle more than one thing here today."

"You sidin' with this here horse thief?" Dorfman demanded.

"I'm sidin' nobody. Last night you hanged a man. You're going to produce evidence here today as to why you believed him guilty. If that evidence isn't good, you'll be tried for murder."

Dorfman's face turned ugly. "Why, you old fool. You can't get away with that. Vetter's sheriff, not you. Besides," he sneered, "you've only got one man with you."

"Two," Loop said quietly. "I'm sidin' Allen . . . and Cat Morgan, too."

Hatred blazed in Dorfman's eyes. "I never seen no good come out of a 'breed yet!" he flared. "You'll answer for this!"

Dave Allen dismounted, keeping his horse

between himself and Dorfman. By that time a good-size crowd had gathered about. Tex Norris wore his gun well to the front, and he kept his eyes roving from one to the other of Dorfman's riders. Cat Morgan watched but said nothing.

Four men had accompanied Dorfman, but there were others here who appeared to belong to his group. With Allen and himself there were only Tex and Loop, and yet, looking at them, he felt suddenly happy. There were no better men than these, Tex with his boyish smile and careful eyes, Loop with his long, serious face. These men would stick. He stepped then into the van, seeing Vetter approach.

Outside their own circle were the townspeople. These, in the last analysis, would be the judges, and now they were saying nothing. Beside him he felt a gentle pressure against his leg and, looking down, saw Jeb standing there. The big dog had never left him. Morgan's heart was suddenly warm and his mind was cool and ready.

"Dorfman!" His voice rang in the street. "Last night you hung my riding partner. Hung him for a horse thief, without evidence or reason. I charge you with murder. The trail you had followed you lost, as Dave Allen and Loop will testify. Then you took it upon yourself to hang an old man simply because he happened to be in the vicinity."

His voice was loud in the street, and not a person in the crowd but could hear every syllable.

Dorfman shifted his feet, his face ugly with anger, yet worried, too. Why didn't Vetter stop him? Arrest him?

"Moreover, the horses you were searching for were stolen by you from Laurie Madison, in Montana. They were taken from the ranch after that ranch had been illegally sold, and after you and Vetter had murdered her father."

"That's a lie!" Dorfman shouted. He was frightened now. There was no telling how far such talk might carry. Once branded, a man would have a lot of explaining to do.

Suppose what Morgan had told Vetter was true? That they were wanted in Montana? Suppose something had been uncovered?

He looked beyond Morgan at Allen, Loop, and Tex. They worried him, for he knew their breed. Dave Allen was an Indian fighter, known and respected. Tex had killed a rustler only a few months ago in a gun battle. Loop was cool, careful, and a dead shot.

"That's a lie," he repeated. "Madison owed me money. I had papers ag'in' him."

"Forged papers. We're reopening the case, Dorfman, and this time there won't be any fixed judge to side you."

Dorfman felt trapped. Twice Cat Morgan had refused to draw when he had named him a liar, but Dorfman knew it was simply because he had not yet had his say. Of many things he was uncertain, but of one he was positive. Cat Morgan was not yellow.

Before he spoke again, Sheriff Ad Vetter suddenly walked into sight. "I been investigatin' your claim," he said to Morgan, "and she won't hold water. The evidence shows you strung up the old man yourself."

Cat Morgan shrugged. "Figured something like that from you, Vetter. What evidence?"

"Nobody else been near the place. That story about a gal is all cock and bull. You had some idea of an alibi when you dragged that in here."

"Why would he murder his partner?" Allen asked quietly. "That ain't sense, Ad."

"They got four lions up there. Them lions are worth money. He wanted it all for himself."

Cat Morgan smiled, and, slowly lifting his left hand, he tilted his hat slightly. "Vetter," he said, "you've got a lot to learn. Lone John was my partner only in the camping and riding. He was working for me. I catch my own cats. I've got a contract with Lone John. Got my copy here in my pocket. He's going to be a hard man to replace because he'd learned how to handle cats. I went up the trees after 'em. Lone John was mighty slick with a rope, and, when a lion hit ground, he dropped a rope on 'em fast. I liked that old man, Sheriff, and I'm charging Dorfman with murder like I said. I want him put in jail . . . now!"

Vetter's face darkened. "You givin' orders?"

35

"If you've got any more evidence against Morgan," Allen interrupted, "trot it out. Remember, I rode with Dorfman on that first posse. I know how he felt about this. He was frettin' to hang somebody, and the beatin' he took didn't set well. He figured Lone John's hangin' would scare Morgan out of the country."

Vetter hesitated, glancing almost apologetically at Dorfman. "Come on, Dorf," he said. "We'll clear you. Come along."

An instant only the rancher hesitated, his eyes ugly. His glance went from Allen back to Cat Morgan, and then he turned abruptly. The two men walked away together. Dave Allen looked worried and he turned to Morgan. "You'd better get some evidence, Cat," he said. "No jury would hang him on this, or even hold him for trial."

It was late evening in the cabin and Laurie filled Cat's cup once more. Outside, the chained big cats prowled restlessly, for Morgan had brought them down to the girl's valley to take better care of them, much to the disgust of Pancho, who stared at them from his perch and scolded wickedly.

"What do you think will happen?" Laurie asked. "Will they come to trial?"

"Not they, just Dorfman. Yes, I've got enough now so that I can prove a fair case against him. I've found a man who will testify that he saw him leave town with four riders and head for the hills, and

36

that was after Allen and that crowd had returned. I've checked that rope they used, and it is Dorfman's. He used a hair rope, and 'most everybody around here uses rawhide reatas. Several folks will swear to that rope."

"Horse thief," Pancho said huskily. "Durned horse thief."

"Be still," Laurie said, turning on the parrot. "You be still!"

Jeb lifted his heavy head and stared curiously, his head cocked at the parrot that looked upon Jeb with almost as much disfavor as the cats.

"These witnesses are all afraid of Dorfman, but, if he is brought to trial, they will testify."

Suddenly Pancho screamed, and Laurie came to her feet, her face pale. From the door there was a dry chuckle. "Don't scream, lady. It's too late for that." It was Ad Vetter's voice.

Cat Morgan sat very still. His back was toward the door, his eyes on Laurie's face. He was thinking desperately.

"Looks like this is the showdown." That was Dorfman's voice. He stepped through the door and shoved the girl. She stumbled back and sat down hard on her chair. "You little fool! You wouldn't take that ticket and money and let well enough alone. You had to butt into trouble. Now you'll die for it, and so will this lion-huntin' friend of yours."

The night was very still. Jeb lay on the floor, his head flattened on his paws, his eyes watching

37

Dorfman. Neither man had seemed to notice the parrot. "Allen will be asking why you let Dorfman out," Morgan suggested, keeping his voice calm.

"He don't know it," Vetter said smugly. "Dorf'll be back in jail afore mornin', and in a few days, when you don't show up as a witness against him, he'll he freed. Your witnesses won't talk unless you get Dorf on trial. They're scared. As for Dave Allen, we'll handle him later, and that 'breed, too."

"Too bad it won't work," Morgan said. Yet even as he spoke, he thought desperately that this was the end. He didn't have a chance. Nobody knew of this place, and the two of them could be murdered here, buried, and probably it would be years before the valley was found. Yet it was Laurie of whom he was thinking now. It would be nothing so easy as murder for her, not to begin with. And knowing the kind of men Dorfman and Vetter were, he could imagine few things worse for any girl than to be left to their mercy.

He made up his mind then. There was no use waiting. No use at all. They would be killed; the time to act was now. He might get one or both of them before they got him. As it was, he was doing nothing, helping none at all.

"You two," he said, "will find yourselves looking through cottonwood leaves at the end of a rope."

"Horse thief!" Pancho screamed. "Durned horse thief!"

Both men wheeled, startled by the unexpected

voice, and Cat left his chair with a lunge. His big shoulder caught Dorfman in the small of the back and knocked him sprawling against the pile of wood beside the stove. Vetter whirled and fired as he turned, but the shot missed, and Morgan caught him with a glancing swing that knocked him sprawling against the far wall. Cat Morgan went after him with a lunge, just as Dorfman scrambled from the wood pile and grabbed for a gun. He heard a fierce growl and whirled just as Jeb hurtled through the air, big jaws agape.

The gun blasted, but the shot was high and Jeb seized the arm in his huge jaws, and then man and dog went rolling over and over on the floor. Vetter threw Morgan off and came to his feet, but Morgan lashed out with a left that knocked him back through the door. Dorfman managed to get away from the dog and sprang through the door just as Ad Vetter came to his feet, grabbing for his gun.

Cat Morgan skidded to a stop, realizing even as his gun flashed up that he was outlined against the lighted door. He felt the gun buck in his hand, heard the thud of Vetter's bullet in the wall beside him, and saw Ad Vetter turn half around and fall on his face. At the same moment a hoarse scream rang out behind the house, and, darting around, Morgan saw a dark figure rolling over and over on the ground among the chained lions!

Grabbing a whip, he sprang among them, and in the space of a couple of breaths had driven the lions back. Then he caught Dorfman and dragged him free of the beasts. Apparently blinded by the sudden rush from light into darkness, and mad to escape from Jeb, the rancher had rushed right into the middle of the lions. Laurie bent over Morgan. "Is . . . is he dead?"

"No. Get some water on, fast. He's living, but he's badly bitten and clawed." Picking up the wounded man, he carried him into the house and placed him on the bed.

Quickly he cut away the torn coat and shirt. Dorfman was unconscious but moaning.

"I'd better go for the doctor," he said.

"There's somebody coming now, Cat. Riders."

Catching up his rifle, Morgan turned to the door. Then he saw Dave Allen, Tex, and Loop with a half dozen other riders. One of the men in a dark coat was bending over the body of Ad Vetter.

"The man who needs you is in here," Morgan said. "Dorfman ran into my lions in the dark."

Dave Allen came to the door. "This clears you, Morgan," he said, "and I reckon a full investigation will get this lady back her ranch, or what money's left, anyway. And full title to her horses. "Loop," he added, "was suspicious. He watched Vetter and saw him slip out with Dorfman, and then got us and we followed them. They stumbled onto your trail here, and we came right after, but we laid back to see what they had in mind."

"Thanks." Cat Morgan glanced over at Laurie, and their eyes met. She moved quickly to him. "I reckon, Allen, we'll file a claim on this valley. Both of us are sort of attached to it."

"Don't blame you. Nice place to build a home."

"That," Morgan agreed, "is what I've been thinking."

The Trail to Peach Meadow Cañon

I

Winter snows were melting in the forests of the Kaibab, and the red-and-orange hue of the 1,000-foot Vermilion Cliffs was streaked with the dampness of melting frost. Deer were feeding in the forest glades among the stands of ponderosa and fir, and the trout were leaping in the streams. Where sunlight trailed through the webbed overhang of the leaves, the water danced and sparkled.

Five deer were feeding on the grass along a mountain stream back of Finger Butte, their coats mottled by the light and shadow of the sun shining through the trees. A vague something moved in the woods behind them, and the five-pronged buck lifted his regal head and stared curiously about. He turned his nose into the wind, reading it cautiously. But his trust was betrayal, for the movement was downwind of him.

The movement came again, and a young man stepped from concealment behind a huge fir not twenty feet from the nearest deer. He was straight and tall in gray, fringed buckskins, and he wore no hat. His hair was thick, black, and wavy, growing fully over the temples, and his face was lean and brown. Smiling, he walked toward the deer with

43

quick, lithe strides, and had taken three full steps before some tiny sound betrayed him.

The buck's head came up and swung around, and then with a startled snort it sprang away, the others following.

Mike Bastian stood grinning, his hands on his hips.

"Well, what do you think now, Roundy?" he called. "Could your Apache beat that? I could have touched him if I had jumped after him!"

Rance Roundy came out of the trees—a lean, wiry old man with a gray mustache and blue eyes that were still bright with an alert awareness.

"No, I'll be darned if any Apache ever lived as could beat that!" he chortled. "Not a mite of it! An' I never seen the day I could beat it, either. You're a caution, Mike, you sure are. I'm glad you're not sneakin' up after *my* hair!" He drew his pipe from his pocket and started stoking it with tobacco. "We're goin' back to Toadstool Cañon, Mike. Your dad sent for us."

Bastian looked up quickly. "Is there trouble, is that it?"

"No, only he wants to talk with you. Maybe"— Roundy was cautious—"he figures it's time you went out on a job. On one of those rides."

"I think that's it." Mike nodded. "He said in the spring, and it's about time for the first ride. I wonder where they'll go this time."

"No tellin'. The deal will be well planned,

44

though. That dad of yours would have made a fine general, Mike. He's got the head for it, he sure has. Never forgets a thing, that one."

"You've been with him a long time, haven't you?"

"Sure . . . since before he found you. I knowed him in Mexico in the war, and that was longer ago than I like to think. I was a boy then, my own self. Son," Roundy said suddenly, "look!"

He tossed a huge pine cone into the air, a big one at least nine inches long.

With a flash of movement, Mike Bastian palmed his gun, and almost as soon as it hit his hand it belched flame—and again. The second shot spattered the cone into a bunch of flying brown chips.

"Not bad!" Roundy nodded. "You still shoot too quick, though. You got to get over that, Mike. Sometimes, one shot is all you'll ever get."

Side-by-side the two walked through the trees, the earth spongy with a thick blanket of pine needles. Roundy was not as tall as Mike, but he walked with the long, springy stride of the woodsman. He smoked in silence for some distance, and then he spoke up.

"Mike, if Ben's ready for you to go out, what will you do?"

For two steps, Bastian said nothing. Then he spoke slowly. "Why, go, I guess. What else?"

"You're sure? You're sure you want to be an outlaw?"

"That's what I was raised for, isn't it?" There was some bitterness in Mike's voice. "Somebody to take over what Ben Curry started?"

"Yeah, that's what you were raised for, all right. But this you want to remember, Mike. It's your life. Ben Curry, for all his power, can't live it for you. Moreover, times have changed since Ben and me rode into this country. It ain't free and wild like it was, because folks are comin' in, settlin' it up, makin' homes. Gettin' away won't be so easy, and your pards will change, too. In fact, they have already changed. When Ben and me come into this country, it was every man for himself. More than one harum-scarum fella, who was otherwise all right, got himself the name of an outlaw. Nobody figured much about it, then. We rustled cows, but so did half the big ranchers of the West. And if a cowpoke got hard up and stopped a stage, nobody made much fuss unless he killed somebody. They figured it was just high spirits. But the last few years, it ain't like that no more. And it ain't only that the country is growin' up . . . it's partly Ben Curry himself."

"You mean he's grown too big?" Mike put in.

"What else? Why, your dad controls more land than there is in New York State. Got it right under his thumb. And he's feared over half the

West by those who knows about him, although not many do.

"Outside of this country around us, nobody ain't seen Ben Curry in years, not leastwise to know him. But they've heard his name, and they know that somewhere an outlaw lives who rules a gang of almost a thousand men. That he robs and rustles where he will, and nobody has nerve enough to chase him.

"He's been smart, just plenty smart," old Roundy went on. "Men ride out and they meet at a given point. The whole job is planned in every detail . . . it's rehearsed, and then they pull it and scatter and meet again here. For a long time folks laid it to driftin' cowpunchers or to gangs passin' through. The way he's set up, one of the gangs he sends out might pull somethin' anywhere from San Antone to Los Angeles, or from Canada to Mexico, although usually he handles it close around.

"He's been the brains, all right, but don't ever forget it was those guns of his that kept things in line. Lately he hasn't used his guns. Kerb Perrin and Rigger Molina or some of their boys handle the discipline. He's become too big, Ben Curry has. He's like a king, and the king isn't gettin' any younger. How do you suppose Perrin will take it when he hears about you takin' over? You think he'll like it?"

"I don't imagine he will," Mike replied

47

thoughtfully. "He's probably done some figuring of his own."

"You bet he has. So has Molina, and neither of them will stop short of murder to get what they want. Your dad still has them buffaloed, I think, but that isn't going to matter when the showdown comes. And I think it's here."

"You do?" Mike said, surprise in his voice.

"Yeah, I sure do. . . ." Roundy hesitated. "You know, Mike, I never told you this, but Ben Curry has a family."

"A *family?*" Despite himself, Mike Bastian was startled.

"Yes, he has a wife and two daughters, and they don't have any idea he's an outlaw. They live down near Tucson somewhere. Occasionally they come to a ranch he owns in Red Wall Cañon, a ranch supposedly owned by Voyle Ragan. He visits them there."

"Does anybody else know this?"

"Not a soul. And don't you be tellin' anybody. You see, Ben always wanted a son, and he never had one. When your real dad was killed down in Mesilla, he took you along with him, and later he told me he was goin' to raise you to take over whatever he left. That was a long time ago, and since then he's spent a sight of time and money on you.

"You can track like an Apache," Roundy said, looking at the tall lad beside him. "In the woods

48

you're a ghost, and I doubt if old Ben Curry himself can throw a gun any faster than you. I'd say you could ride anything that wore hair, and what you don't know about cards, dice, and roulette wheels ain't in it. You can handle a knife and fight with your fists, and you can open anything a man ever made in the way of safes and locks. Along with that, you've had a good education, and you could take care of yourself in any company. I don't reckon there ever was a boy had the kind of education you got, and I think Ben's ready to retire."

"You mean . . . to join his wife and daughters?" Mike questioned.

"That's it. He's gettin' no younger, and he wants it easy-like for the last years. He was always scared of only one thing, and he had a lot of it as a youngster. That's poverty. Well, he's made his pile, and now he wants to step out. Still and all, he knows he can't get out alive unless he leaves somebody behind him that's strong enough and smart enough to keep things under control. That's where you come in."

"Why don't he let Perrin have it?"

"Mike, you know Perrin. He's dangerous, that one. He's poison mean and power crazy. He'd have gone off the deep end a long time ago if it wasn't for Ben Curry. And Rigger Molina is kill crazy. He would have killed fifty men if it hadn't been that he knew Ben Curry would kill him when he got back. No, neither of them could handle this outfit. The whole shebang would go to pieces in ninety days if they had it."

Mike Bastian walked along in silence. There was little that was new in what Roundy was saying, but he was faintly curious as to the old man's purpose. The pair had been much together, and they knew each other as few men ever did. They had gone through storm and hunger and thirst together, living in the desert, mountains, and forest, only rarely returning to the rendezvous in Toadstool Cañon.

Roundy had a purpose in his talking, and Bastian waited, listening. Yet even as he walked, he was conscious of everything that went on around him. A quail had moved back into the tall grass near the stream, and there was a squirrel up ahead in the crotch of a tree. Not far back a gray wolf had crossed the path only minutes ahead of them.

It was as Roundy had said. Mike was a woodsman, and the thought of taking over the outlaw band filled him with unease. Always, he had been aware this time would come, that he had been schooled for it. But before, it had seemed remote and far off. Now, suddenly, it was at hand; it was facing him.

"Mike," Roundy went on, "the country is growin' up. Last spring some of our raids raised merry hell, and some of the boys had a bad time gettin' away. When they start again, there will be trouble and lots of it. Another thing, folks don't look at an outlaw like they used to. He isn't just a wild young cowhand full of liquor, nor a fellow who needs a poke, nor somebody buildin' a spread of his own. Now, he'll be like a wolf, with every man huntin' him. Before you decide to go into this, you think it over, make up your own mind.

"You know Ben Curry, and I know you like him. Well, you should. Nevertheless, Ben had no right to raise you for an outlaw. He went his way of his own free will, and, if he saw it that way, that was his own doin'. But no man has a right to say to another . . . 'This you must do . . . this you must be.' No man has a right to train another, startin' before he has a chance to make up his mind, and school him in any particular way."

The old man stopped to relight his pipe, and Mike kept a silence, would let Roundy talk out what seemed to bother him.

"I think every man should have the right to decide his own destiny, insofar as he can," Roundy said, continuing his trend of thought. "That goes for you, Mike, and you've got the decision ahead of you. I don't know which you'll do. But if you decide to step out of this gang, then I don't relish bein' around when it happens, for old Ben will be fit to be tied.

"Right now, you're an honest man. You're clean as a whistle. Once you become an outlaw, a lot of things will change. You'll have to kill, too . . .

51

don't forget that. It's one thing to kill in defense of your home, your family, or your country. It's another thing when you kill for money or for power."

"You think I'd have to kill Perrin and Molina?" Mike Bastian asked.

"If they didn't get you first!" Roundy spat. "Don't forget this, Mike, you're fast. You're one of the finest and, aside from Ben Curry, probably the finest shot I ever saw. But that ain't shootin' at a man who's shootin' at you. There's a powerful lot of difference, as you'll see.

"Take Billy the Kid, this Lincoln County gunman we hear about. Frank and George Coe, Dick Brewer, Jesse Evans . . . any one of them can shoot as good as him. The difference is that the part down inside of him where the nerves should be was left out. When he starts shootin' and when he's bein' shot at, he's like ice! Kerb Perrin's that way, too. Perrin's the cold type, steady as a rock. Rigger Molina's another kind of cat . . . he explodes all over the place. He's white-hot, but he's deadly as a rattler."

Mike was listening intently as Roundy continued his description: "Five of them cornered him one time at a stage station out of Julesburg. When the shootin' was over, four of them were down and the fifth was holdin' a gunshot arm. Molina, he rode off under his own power. He's a shaggy wolf, that one. Wild and uncurried and big as a bear."

Far more than Roundy realized did Mike Bastian know the facts about Ben Curry's empire of crime. For three years now, Curry had been leading his foster son through all the intricate maze of his planning. There were spies and agents in nearly every town in the Southwest, and small groups of outlaws quartered here and there on ranches who could be called upon for help at a moment's notice.

Also, there were ranches where fresh horses could be had, and changes of clothing, and where the horses the band had ridden could be lost. At Toadstool Cañon were less than 200 of the total number of outlaws, and many of those, while living under Curry's protection, were not of his band.

Also, the point Roundy raised had been in Mike's mind, festering there, an abscess of doubt and dismay. The Ben Curry he knew was a huge, kindly man, even if grim and forbidding at times. He had taken the homeless boy and given him kindness and care, had, indeed, trained him as a son. Today, however, was the first inkling Mike had of the existence of that other family. Ben Curry had planned and acted with shrewdness and care.

Mike Bastian had a decision to make, a decision that would change his entire life, whether for better or worse.

Here in the country around the Vermilion Cliffs was the only world he knew. Beyond it? Well, he supposed he could punch cows. He was trained to do many things, and probably there were jobs awaiting such a man as himself.

He could become a gambler, but he had seen and known a good many gamblers and did not relish the idea. Somewhere beyond this wilderness was a larger, newer, wealthier land—a land where honest men lived and reared their families.

II

In the massive stone house at the head of Toadstool Cañon, so called because of the gigantic toadstool-like stone near the entrance, Ben Curry leaned his great weight back in his chair and stared broodingly out the door over the valley below.

His big face was blunt and unlined as rock, but the shock of hair above his leonine face was turning to gray. He was growing old. Even spring did not bring the old fire to his veins again, and it had been long since he had ridden out on one of the jobs he planned so shrewdly. It was time he quit.

Yet this man, who had made decisions sharply and quickly, was for the first time in his life uncertain. For six years he had ruled supreme in this remote corner north of the Colorado. For twenty years he had been an outlaw, and for fifteen of those twenty years he had ruled a gang that had grown and extended its ramifications until it was an empire in itself.

Six years ago he had moved to this remote country and created the stronghold where he now lived. Across the southern limit rolled the Colorado River, with its long cañons and maze of rocky wilderness, a bar to any pursuit from the country south of the river, where he operated.

As far as other men were concerned, only at Lee's Ferry was there a crossing, and, in a cabin nearby, his men watched it night and day. In fact, there were two more crossings—one that the gang used in going to and from their raids, and the other known only to himself. It was his ace in the hole, even if not his only one.

One law of the gang, never transgressed, was that there was to be no lawless activity in the Mormon country to the north of them. The Mormons and the Indians were left strictly alone and were their friends. So were the few ranchers who lived in the area. These few traded at the stores run by the gang, buying their supplies closer to home and at cheaper prices than they could have managed elsewhere.

Ben Curry had never quite made up his mind about Kerb Perrin. He knew that Perrin was growing restive, that he was aware that Curry was aging and was eager for the power of leadership. Yet the one factor Curry couldn't be certain about was whether Perrin would stand for the taking over of the band by Mike Bastian.

Well, Mike had been well trained; it would be his

problem. Ben smiled grimly. He was the old bull of the herd, and Perrin was pawing the dirt, but what would he say when a young bull stepped in? One who had not won his spurs with the gang?

That was why Curry had sent for him, for it was time Mike be groomed for leadership, time he moved out on his first job. And he had just the one. It was big, it was sudden, and it was dramatic. It would have an excellent effect on the gang if it was brought off smoothly, and he was going to let Mike plan the whole job himself.

There was a sharp knock outside, and Curry smiled a little, recognizing it.

"Come in!" he bellowed.

He watched Perrin stride into the room with his quick, nervous steps, his eyes scanning the room.

"Chief," Perrin said, "the boys are gettin' restless. It's spring, you know, and most of them are broke. Have you got anything in mind?"

"Sure, several things. But one that's good and tough. Struck me it might be a good one to break the kid in on."

"Oh?" Perrin's eyes veiled. "You mean he'll go along?"

"No, I'm going to let him run it. The whole show. It will be good for him."

Kerb Perrin absorbed that. For the first time, he felt worry. For the first time, an element of doubt entered his mind. He had wondered before about Bastian and what his part would be in all this.

For years, Perrin had looked forward to the time when he could take over. He knew there would be trouble with Rigger Molina, but he had thought out that phase of it. He knew he could handle it. But what if Curry was planning to jump young Bastian into leadership?

Quick, hot passion surged through Perrin, and, when he looked up, it was all he could do to keep his voice calm.

"You think that's wise?" he questioned. "How will the boys feel about goin' out with a green kid?"

"He knows what to do," Curry said. "They'll find he's smart as any of them, and he knows plenty. This is a big job, and a tough one."

"Who goes with him?"

"Maybe I'll let him pick them," Curry said thoughtfully. "Good practice for him."

"What's the job?" Perrin asked, voice sullen.

"The gold train."

Perrin's fingers tightened, digging into his palms. This was the job *he* wanted! The shipment from the mines! It would be enormous, rich beyond anything they had done!

Months before, in talking of this job, he had laid out his plan for it before Curry. But it had been vetoed. He had recommended the killing of every man jack of them, and burial of them all, so the train would vanish completely.

"You sound like Molina," Curry had said, chuckling. "Too bloody."

"Dead men don't talk," he had replied grimly.

Yet, even as he spoke, he was thinking of something else. He was thinking of the effect of this upon the men of the outfit. He knew many of them liked Mike Bastian, and more than one of them had helped train him. In a way, many of the older men were as proud of Mike as if he had been their own son. If he stepped out now and brought off this job, he would acquire power and prestige in the gang equal to Perrin's own.

Fury engulfed Perrin. Curry had no right to do this to him! Sidetracking him for an untried kid. Shoving Bastian down all their throats.

Suddenly the rage died, and in its place came resolution. It was time he acted on his own. He would swing his own job, the one he had had in mind for so long, and that would counteract the effect of the gold-train steal. Moreover, he would be throwing the challenge into Ben Curry's teeth, for he would plan this job without consulting him. If there was going to be a struggle for leadership, it could begin here and now.

"He'll handle the job, all right," Curry said confidently. "He has been trained, and he has the mind for it. He plans well. I hadn't spoken of it before, but I asked his advice on a few things without letting him know why, and he always came through with the right answers."

Kerb Perrin left the stone house filled with burning resentment but also something of triumph.

At last, after years of taking orders, he was going on his own. Yet the still, small voice of fear was in him, too. *What would Ben Curry do?*

The thought made him quail. He had seen the cold fury of Curry when it was aroused, and he had seen him use a gun. He himself was fast, but was he as fast as Ben Curry? In his heart, he doubted it. He dismissed the thought, although storing it in his mind. Something would have to be done about Ben Curry. . . .

Mike Bastian stood before Ben Curry's table, and the two men stared at each other.

Ben Curry, the old outlaw chief, was huge, bear-like, and mighty, his eyes fierce yet glowing with a kindly light now, and something of pride, too. Facing him, tall and lithe, his shoulders broad and mighty, was Mike Bastian, child of the frontier, grown to manhood and trained in every art of the wilds, every dishonest practice in the books, every skill with weapons. Yet educated, too, a man who could conduct himself well in any company.

"You take four men and look over the ground yourself, Mike," Ben Curry was saying. "I want you to plan this one. The gold train leaves the mines on the Twentieth. There will be five wagons, the gold distributed among them, although there won't be a lot of it as far as quantity is concerned. That gold train will be worth roughly five hundred thousand dollars.

"When that job is done," he continued, "I'm going to step down and leave you in command. You knew I was planning that. I'm old, and I want to live quietly for a while, and this outfit takes a strong hand to run it. Think you can handle it?"

"I think so," Mike Bastian said softly.

"I think so, too. Watch Perrin . . . he's the snaky one. Rigger is dangerous, but whatever he does will be out in the open. Not so Perrin. He's a conniver. He never got far with me because I was always one jump ahead of him. And I still am."

The old man was silent for a few minutes as he stared out the window.

"Mike," he said then, doubt entering his voice, "maybe I've done wrong. I meant to raise you the way I have. I ain't so sure what is right and wrong, and never was. Never gave it much thought, though.

"When I come West, it was dog eat dog, and your teeth had to be big. I got knocked down and kicked around some, and then I started taking big bites myself. I organized, and then I got bigger. In all these years nobody has ever touched me. If *you've* got a strong hand, you can do the same. Sometimes you'll have to buy men, sometimes you'll have to frighten them, and sometimes you'll have to kill."

He shook his head as if clearing it of memories past, and then glanced up.

"Who will you take with you?" he asked. "I mean, in scouting this layout?"

Ben Curry waited, for it was judgment of men that Bastian would need most. It pleased him that Mike did not hesitate.

"Roundy, Doc Sawyer, Colley, and Garlin."

Curry glanced at him, his eyes hard and curious. "Why?"

"Roundy has an eye for terrain like no man in this world," Mike said. "He says mine's as good, but I'll take him along to verify or correct my judgment. Doc Sawyer is completely honest. If he thinks I'm wrong, he'll say so. As for Colley and Garlin, they are two of the best men in the whole outfit. They will be pleased that I ask their help, which puts them on my side in a measure, and they can see how I work."

Curry nodded. "Smart . . . and you're right. Colley and Garlin are two of the best men, and absolutely fearless." He smiled a little. "If you have trouble with Perrin or Molina, it won't hurt to have them on your side."

Despite himself, Mike Bastian was excited. He was twenty-two years old and by frontier standards had been a man for several years. But in all that time, aside from a few trips into the Mormon country and one to Salt Lake, he had never been out of the maze of cañons and mountains north of the Colorado.

Roundy led the way, for the trail was an old one to him. They were taking the secret route south used by the gang on their raids, and, as they rode toward it, Mike stared at the country. He was always astonished by its ruggedness.

Snow still lay in some of the darker places of the forest, but as they neared the cañon, the high cliffs towered even higher and the trail dipped down through a narrow gorge of rock. Countless centuries of erosion had carved the rock into grotesque figures resembling those of men and animals, colored with shades of brown, pink, gray, and red, and tapering off into a pale yellow. There were shadowed pools among the rocks, some from snow water and others from natural springs, and there were scattered clumps of oak and piñon.

In the bottom of the gorge the sun did not penetrate except at high noon and there the trail wound along between great jumbled heaps of boulders, cracked and broken from their fall off the higher cliffs.

Mike Bastian followed Roundy, who rode hump-shouldered on a ragged, gray horse that seemed as old as he himself but also as sure-footed and mountain-wise. Mike was wearing a black hat now, but his same buckskins. He had substituted boots for the moccasins he usually wore, although they reposed in his saddlebags, ready at hand.

Behind them rode Doc Sawyer, his lean, saturnine face quiet, his eyes faintly curious and interested as he scanned the massive walls of the cañon. Tubby Colley was short and thick-chested, and very confident—a hard-jawed man who had been a first-rate ranch foreman before he shot two men and hit the outlaw trail.

Tex Garlin was tall, rangy, and quiet. He was a Texan, and little else was known of his background, although it was said he could carve a dozen notches on his guns if he had wished.

Suddenly Roundy turned the gray horse and rode abruptly at the face of the cliff, but when he came close up, the sand and boulders broke and a path showed along the under-scoured rock. Following this for several hundred yards, they found a cañon that cut back into the cliff itself and then turned to head toward the river.

The roar of the Colorado, high with spring freshets, was loud in their ears before they reached it. Finally they came out on a sandy bank littered with driftwood.

Nearby was a small cabin and a plot of garden. The door of the house opened, and a tall old man came out.

"Howdy!" he said. "I been expectin' somebody." His shrewd old eyes glanced from face to face, and then hesitated at sight of Mike. "Ain't seen you before," he said pointedly.

"It's all right, Bill," Roundy said. "This is Mike Bastian."

"Ben Curry's boy?" Bill stared. "I heard a sight of you, son. I sure have! Can you shoot like they say?"

Mike flushed. "I don't know what they say," he said, grinning. "But I'll bet a lot of money I can hit the side of that mountain if it holds still."

Garlin stared at him thoughtfully, and Colley smiled a little.

"Don't take no funnin' from him," Roundy said. "That boy can shoot."

"Let's see some shootin, son," Bill suggested. "I always did like to see a man who could shoot."

Bastian shook his head. "There's no reason for shootin'," he protested. "A man's a fool to shoot unless he's got cause. Ben Curry always told me never to draw a gun unless I meant to use it."

"Go ahead," Colley said. "Show him."

Old Bill pointed. "See that black stick end juttin' up over there? It's about fifty, maybe sixty paces. Can you hit it?"

"You mean that one?" Mike palmed his gun and fired, and the black stick pulverized.

It was a movement so smooth and practiced that no one of the men even guessed he had intended to shoot. Garlin's jaws stopped their calm chewing, and he stared with his mouth open for as long as it took to draw a breath. Then he glanced at Colley.

"Wonder what Kerb would say to that?" he said, astonished. "This kid can shoot."

"Yeah," Colley agreed, "but the stick didn't have a gun."

Old Bill worked the ferry out of a cave under the cliff and freighted them across the swollen river in one hair-raising trip. With the river behind, they wound up through the rocks and started south.

III

The mining and cow town of Weaver was backed up near a large hill on the banks of a small creek. Colley and Garlin rode into the place at sundown, and an hour later Doc Sawyer and Roundy rode in.

Garlin and Colley were leaning on the bar having a drink, and they ignored the newcomers. Mike Bastian followed not long afterward and walked to the bar alone.

All the others in the saloon were Mexicans, except for three tough-looking white men lounging against the bar nearby. They glanced at Mike and his buckskins, and one of them whispered something to the others, at which they all laughed.

Doc Sawyer was sitting in a poker game, and his eyes lifted. Mike leaned nonchalantly against the bar, avoiding the stares of the three toughs who stood near him. One of them moved over closer.

"Hi, stranger," he said. "That's a right purty suit you got. Where could I get one like it?"

Garlin looked up and his face stiffened. He nudged Colley. "Look," Garlin said quickly.

"Corbus and Fletcher. An' trouble huntin'. We'd better get into this."

Colley shook his head. "No. Let's see what the kid does."

Mike looked around, his expression mild. "You want a suit like this?" he inquired of the stranger. His eyes were innocent, but he could see the sort of man he had to deal with. These three were toughs, and dangerous. " 'Most any Navajo could make one for you."

"Just like that?" Corbus sneered.

He was drinking and in a nagging, quarrelsome mood. Mike looked altogether too neat for his taste.

"Sure. Just like this," Mike agreed. "But I don't know what you'd want with it, though. This suit would be pretty big for you to fill."

"Huh?" Corbus's face flamed. Then his mouth tightened. "You gettin' smart with me, kid?"

"No." Mike Bastian turned, and his voice cracked like a whip in the suddenly silent room. "Neither am I being hurrahed by any lame-brained, liquor-guzzling saddle tramp. You made a remark about my suit, and I answered it. Now, you can have a drink on me, all three of you, and I'm suggesting you drink up." His voice suddenly became soft. "I want you to drink up because I want to be very, very sure we're friends, see?"

Corbus stared at Bastian, a cold hint of danger filtering through the normal stubbornness of his

66

brain. Something told him this was perilous going, yet he was stubborn, too stubborn. He smiled slowly. "Kid," he drawled, "supposin' I don't want to drink with no tenderfoot brat?"

Corbus never saw what happened. His brain warned him as Mike's left hand moved, but he never saw the right. The left stabbed his lips and the right cracked on the angle of his jaw, and he lifted from his feet and hit the floor on his shoulder blades, out cold.

Fletcher and the third tough stared from Corbus to Mike. Bastian was not smiling. "You boys want to drink?" he asked. "Or do we go on from here?"

Fletcher stared at him. "What if a man drawed a gun instead of usin' his fists?" he demanded.

"I'd kill him," Bastian replied quietly.

Fletcher blinked. "I reckon you would," he agreed. He turned and said: "Let's have a drink. That Boot Hill out there's already got twenty graves in it."

Garlin glanced at Colley, his eyebrows lifted. Colley shrugged.

"I wonder what Corbus will do when he gets up?" he said.

Garlin chuckled. "Nothin' today. He won't be feelin' like it."

Colley nodded. "Reckon you're right, an' I reckon the old man raised him a wildcat. I can hardly wait to see Kerb Perrin's face when we tell him."

"You reckon," Garlin asked, "that what we heard is true? That Ben Curry figures to put this youngster into his place when he steps out?"

"Yep, that's the talk," Colley answered.

"Well, maybe he's got it. We'll sure know before this trip is over."

Noise of the stagecoach rolling down the street drifted into the saloon, and Mike Bastian strolled outside and started toward the stage station. The passengers were getting down to stretch their legs and to eat. Three of them were women.

One of them noticed Mike standing there and walked toward him. She was a pale, pretty girl with large gray eyes.

"How much farther to Red Wall Cañon?" she inquired.

Mike Bastian stiffened. "Why, not far. That is, you'll make it by morning if you stick with the stage. There is a cross-country way if you had you a buckboard, though."

"Could you tell us where we could hire one? My mother is not feeling well."

He stepped down off the boardwalk and headed toward the livery stable with her. As they drew alongside the stage, Mike looked up. An older woman and a girl were standing near the stage, but he was scarcely aware of anything but the girl. Her hair was blonde, but darker than that of the girl who walked beside him, and her eyes, too, were gray. There the resemblance ended, for where this girl beside him was quiet and sweet, the other was vivid.

She looked at him, and their eyes met. He swept off his hat. The girl beside him spoke.

"This is my mother, Missus Ragan, and my sister Drusilla." She looked up at him quickly. "My name is Juliana."

Mike bowed. He had eyes only for Drusilla, who was staring at him.

"I am Mike Bastian," he said.

"He said he could hire us a rig to drive across country to Red Wall Cañon," Juliana explained. "It will be quicker that way."

"Yes," Mike agreed, "much quicker. I'll see what I can do. Just where in Red Wall did you wish to go?"

"To Voyle Ragan's ranch," Drusilla said. "The V Bar." He had turned away, but he stopped in midstride. "Did you say . . . Voyle Ragan's?"

"Yes. Is there anything wrong?" Drusilla stared at him. "What's the matter?"

He regained his composure swiftly. "Nothing. Only, I'd heard the name, and . . ."—he smiled—"I sort of wanted to know for sure, so if I came calling. . . ."

Juliana laughed. "Why, of course. We'd be glad to see you."

He walked swiftly away. These, then, were Ben Curry's daughters! That older woman would be his wife! He was their foster brother, yet obviously his name had meant nothing to them. Neither, he reflected, would their names have meant anything to him, nor the destination, had it not been for what Roundy had told him only the previous day.

Drusilla her name was. His heart pounded at the memory of her, and he glanced back through the gathering dusk at the three women standing there by the stage station.

Hiring the rig was a matter of minutes. He liked the look of the driver, a lean man, tall and white-haired. "No danger on that road this time of year," the driver said. "I can have them there in no time by takin' the cañon road."

Drusilla was waiting for him when Mike walked back. "Did you find one?" she asked, and then listened to his explanation and thanked him.

"Would it be all right with you," Mike said, "if I call at the V Bar?"

She looked at him, her face grave, but a dancing light in her eyes. "Why, my sister invited you, did she not?"

"Yes, but I'd like you to invite me, too."

"I?" She studied him for a minute. "Of course, we'd be glad to see you. My mother likes visitors as well as Julie and I, so won't you ask her, too?"

"I'll take the invitation from you and your sister as being enough." He grinned. "If I ask your mother, I might have to ask your father."

"Father isn't with us." She laughed. "We'll see him at Ragan's. He's a rancher somewhere up north in the wilds. His name is Ben Ragan. Have you heard of him?"

"Seems to me I have," he admitted, "but I wouldn't say for sure."

After they had gone, Mike wandered around and stopped in the saloon, after another short talk with a man at the livery stable. Listening and asking an occasional question, he gathered the information he wanted on the gold shipment. Even as he asked the questions, it seemed somehow fantastic that he, of all people, should be planning such a thing.

Never before had he thought of it seriously, but now he did. And it was not only because the thought went against his own grain, but because he was thinking of Drusilla Ragan.

What a girl she was! He sobered suddenly. Yet, for all of that, she was the daughter of an outlaw. Did she know it? From her question, he doubted it very much.

Doc Sawyer cashed in his chips and left the poker game to join Mike at the bar.

"The Twentieth, all right," he said softly. "And five of them are going to carry shotguns. There will be twelve guards in all, which looks mighty tough. The big fellow at the poker table is one of the guards, and all of them are picked men."

Staring at his drink, Mike puzzled over his problem. What Roundy had said was of course true. This was a turning point for him. He was still an honest man; yet, when he stepped over the boundary, it would make a difference. It might make a lot of difference to a girl like Dru Ragan, for instance.

The fact that her father, also, was an outlaw would make little difference. Listening to Sawyer made him wonder. Why had such a man, brilliant, intelligent, and well-educated, ever become a criminal?

Sawyer was a gambler and a very skillful one, yet he was a doctor, too, and a fine surgeon. His education was as good as study and money could make it, and it had been under his guidance that Mike Bastian had studied.

"Doc," he said suddenly, "whatever made you ride a crooked trail?"

Sawyer glanced at him suddenly, a new expression in his eyes. "What do you mean, Mike? Do you have doubts?"

"Doubts? That seems to be all I do have these last few days."

"I wondered about that," Doc said. "You have been so quiet that I never doubted but what you were perfectly willing to go on with Ben Curry's plans for you. It means power and money, Mike . . . all a man could want. If it is doubt about the future for outlaws that disturbs you, don't let it. From now on it will be political connections and bribes, but with the money you'll have to work with, that should be easy."

"It should be," Mike said slowly. "Only maybe . . . just maybe . . . I don't want to."

"Conscience rears its ugly head." Sawyer smiled ironically. "Can it be that Ben Curry's instructions have fallen on fallow ground? What started this sudden feeling? The approach of a problem? Fear?" Doc had turned toward Mike and was staring at him with aroused interest. "Or," he added, "is there a woman? A girl?"

"Would that be so strange?"

"Strange? No. I've wondered it hasn't happened before, but then you've lived like a recluse these past years. Who is she?"

"It doesn't matter," Mike answered. "I was thinking of this before I saw her. Wondering what I should do."

"Don't ask me," Sawyer said. "I made a mess of my own life. Partly a woman and partly the desire for what I thought was easy money. Well, there's no such a thing as easy money, but I found that out too late. You make your own decision. What was it Matthew Arnold said? I think you learned the quotation."

" 'No man can save his brother's soul, or pay his brother's debt.' "

"Right. So you save your own and pay your own. There's one thing to remember, Mike. No matter which way you go, there will be killing. If you take over Ben Curry's job, you'll have to kill Perrin and Molina, if you can. And you may have

73

to kill them, and even Ben Curry, if you step out."

"Not Dad," Mike said.

"Don't be so sure. It isn't only what he thinks that matters, Mike. No man is a complete ruler or dictator. His name is only the symbol. He is the mouthpiece for the wishes of his followers, and, as long as he expresses those wishes, he leads them. When he fails, he falls. Ben Curry is the boss not only because he has power in him, but also because he has organization, because he has made them money, because he has offered them safety. If you left, there would be a chink in the armor. No outlaw ever trusts another outlaw who turns honest, for he always fears betrayal."

Bastian tossed off his drink. "Let's check with Roundy. He's been on the prowl."

Roundy came to them hastily. "We've got to get out of town quick," he said. "Ducrow and Fernandez just blew in, and they are drunk and raisin' the devil. Both of them are talkin', too, and, if they see us, they will spill everything."

"All right." Mike straightened. "Get our horses. Get theirs, too. We'll take them with us."

Garlin and Colley had come to the bar. Garlin shook his head. "Ducrow's poison mean when he's drunk, and Fernandez sides him in everything," Garlin informed. "When Ducrow gets drunk, he always pops off too much. The boss forbade him weeks ago to come down here."

"He's a pal of Perrin's," Colley said, "so he thinks he can get away with it."

"Here they come now!" Roundy exclaimed.

"All right . . . drift," Bastian ordered. "Make it quick with the horses."

IV

Saloon doors slammed open, and the two men came in. One look, and Mike could see there was cause for worry. Tom Ducrow was drunk and ugly, and behind him was Snake Fernandez. They were an unpleasant pair, and they had made their share of trouble in Ben Curry's organization, although always protected by Perrin.

Bastian started forward, but he had scarcely taken a step when Ducrow saw him.

"There he is!" he bellowed loudly. "The pet! The boss' pet!" He stared around at the people in the barroom. "You know who this man is? He's. . . ."

"Ducrow!" Mike snapped. "Shut up and go home. Now!"

"Look who's givin' orders!" Ducrow sneered. "Gettin' big for your britches, ain't you?"

"Your horses will be outside in a minute," Mike said. "Get on them and start back, fast!"

"Suppose," Ducrow sneered, "you make me!"

Mike had been moving toward him, and now

with a panther-like leap he was beside the outlaw and, with a quick slash from his pistol barrel, floored him.

With an oath, Snake Fernandez reached for a gun, and Mike had no choice. He shot him in the shoulder. Fernandez staggered, the gun dropping from his fingers. Mouthing curses, he reached for his left-hand gun.

But even as he reached, Garlin—who had stayed behind when the others went for the horses—stepped up behind him. Jerking the gun from the man's holster, he spun him about and shoved him through the door.

Mike pulled the groggy Ducrow to his feet and pushed him outside after Fernandez.

A big man got up hastily from the back of the room. Mike took one quick glimpse at the star on his chest. "What goes on here?" the sheriff demanded.

"Nothing at all," Mike said affably. "Just a couple of the boys from our ranch feeling their oats a little. We'll take them out and off your hands."

The sheriff stared from Mike to Doc Sawyer and Colley, who had just come through the door.

"Who are you?" he demanded. "I don't believe I know you *hombres*."

"That's right, sir, you don't," Mike said. "We're from the Mogollons, riding back after driving some cattle through to California. It was a rough trip, and this liquor here got to a couple of the boys."

The sheriff hesitated, looking sharply from one to the other.

"*You* may be a cowhand," he said, "but that *hombre*"—he pointed to Sawyer—"looks like a gambler."

Mike chuckled. "That's a joke on you, boy!" he said to Doc. Then he turned back to the sheriff. "He's a doctor, sir, and quite a good one. A friend of my boss'."

A gray-haired man got up and strolled alongside the sheriff. His eyes were alive with suspicion.

"From the Mogollons?" he queried. "That's where I'm from. Who did you say your boss was?"

Doc Sawyer felt his scalp tighten, but Mike smiled.

"Jack McCardle," he said, "of the Flying M. We aren't his regular hands, just a bunch passing through. Doc, here, he being an old friend of Jack's, handled the sale of the beef."

The sheriff looked around.

"That right, Joe?" he asked the gray-haired man. "There's a Flying M over there?"

"Yes, there is." Joe was obviously puzzled. "Good man, too, but I had no idea he was shipping beef."

The sheriff studied Bastian thoughtfully. "Guess you're all right," he said finally. "But you sure don't *talk* like a cowhand."

"As a matter of fact," Mike said, swallowing hard, "I was studying for the ministry, but my interests began to lead me in more profane directions, so I am afraid I backslid. It seems," he said gravely, "that a leaning toward poker isn't conducive to the correct manner in the pulpit."

"I should say not." The sheriff chuckled. "All right, son, you take your pardners with you. Let 'em sleep it off."

Mike turned, and his men followed him. Ducrow and Fernandez had disappeared. They rode swiftly out of town and took the trail for Toadstool Cañon. It wasn't until they were several miles on the road that Sawyer glanced at Mike.

"You'll do," he said. "I was never so sure of a fight in my life."

"That's right, boss," Garlin said. "I was bettin' we'd have to shoot our way out of town. You sure smooth-talked 'em. Never heard it done prettier."

"Sure did," Colley agreed. "I don't envy you havin' Ducrow an' Fernandez for enemies, though."

Kerb Perrin and Rigger Molina were both in conference with Ben Curry when Mike Bastian came up the stone steps and through the door. They both looked up sharply.

"Perrin," Bastian said, "what were Ducrow and Fernandez doing in Weaver?"

78

"In Weaver?" Perrin straightened up slowly, nettled by Mike's tone, but puzzled, too.

"Yes, in Weaver. We nearly had to shoot our way out of town because of them. They were down there, drunk and talking too much. When I told them to get on their horses and go home, they made trouble."

Kerb Perrin was on dangerous ground. He well knew how harsh Ben Curry was about talkative outlaws, and, while he had no idea what the two were doing in Weaver, he knew they were troublemakers. He also knew they were supporters of his. Ben Curry knew it, and so did Rigger Molina.

"They made trouble?" Perrin questioned now. "How?"

"Ducrow started to tell who I was."

"What happened?"

Mike was aware that Ben Curry had tipped back in his chair and was watching him with interest.

"I knocked him down with a pistol barrel," he said.

"You *what?*" Perrin stared. Ducrow was a bad man to tangle with. "What about Fernandez?"

"He tried to draw on me, and I put a bullet in his shoulder."

"You should've killed him," Molina said. "You'll have to, sooner or later."

Kerb Perrin was stumped. He had not expected this, or that Mike Bastian was capable of handling such a situation. He was suddenly aware that Doc Sawyer had come into the room.

Bastian faced Ben Curry. "We got what we went after," he said, "but another bad break like Ducrow and Fernandez, and we'd walk into a trap."

"There won't be another." Curry said harshly.

When Mike had gone out, Doc Sawyer looked at Ben Curry and smiled.

"You should have seen him and heard him," he said as Molina and Perrin were leaving. "It would have done your heart good. He had a run-in with Corbus and Fletcher, too. Knocked Corbus out with a punch and backed Fletcher down. Oh, he'll do, that boy of yours, he'll do. The way he talked that sheriff out of it was one of the smoothest things I've seen."

Ben Curry nodded with satisfaction. "I knew it. I knew he had it."

Doc Sawyer smiled, and looked up at the chief from under his sunburned eyebrows. "He met a girl, too."

"A girl? Good for him. It's about time."

"This was a very particular girl, chief," Sawyer continued. "I thought you'd like to know. If I'm any judge of men, he fell for her and fell hard. And I'm not so sure it didn't happen both ways. He told me something about it, but I had already seen for myself."

Something in Sawyer's tone made Curry sit up a little. "Who was the girl?" he demanded.

"A girl who came in on the stage." Doc spoke carefully, avoiding Curry's eyes now. "He got the girl and her family a rig to drive them out to a ranch. Out to the V Bar."

Ben Curry's face went white. So Doc knew! It was in every line of him, every tone of his voice. The one thing he had tried to keep secret, the thing known only to himself and Roundy, was known to Doc! And to how many others?

"The girl's name," Doc continued, "was Drusilla Ragan. She's a beautiful girl."

"Well, I won't have it," Curry said in a strained voice.

Doc Sawyer looked up, faintly curious. "You mean the foster son you raised isn't good enough for your daughter?"

"Don't say that word here!" Curry snapped, his face hard. "Who knows besides you?"

"Nobody of whom I am aware," Doc said with a shrug. "I only know by accident. You will remember the time you were laid up with that bullet wound. You were delirious, and that's why I took care of you myself . . . because you talked too much." Doc lighted his pipe. "They made a nice-looking pair," he said. "And I think she invited him to Red Wall Cañon."

"He won't go! I won't have any of this crowd going there!"

"Chief, that boy's what you made him, but he's not an outlaw yet," Doc said, puffing contentedly on his pipe. "He could be, and he might be, but if he does become one, the crime will lie on your shoulders."

Curry shook himself and stared out the window.

"I said it, chief, the boy has it in him," Sawyer went on. "You should have seen him throw that gun on Fernandez. The kid's fast as lightning. He thinks, too. If he takes over this gang, he'll run this country like you never ran it. I say *if*. . . ."

"He'll do it," Curry said confidently, "you know he will. He always does what I tell him."

Doc chuckled. "He may, and again he may not. Mike Bastian has a mind of his own, and he's doing some thinking. He may decide he doesn't want to take over. What will you do then?"

"Nobody has ever quit this gang. Nobody ever will!"

"You'd order him killed?"

Ben Curry hesitated. This was something he had never dreamed of, something. . . . "He'll do what he's told," he repeated, but he was no longer sure.

A tiny voice of doubt was arising within him, a voice that made him remember the Mike Bastian who was a quiet, determined little boy who would not cry, a boy who listened and obeyed. Yet now Curry knew, and admitted it for the first time, that Mike Bastian always had a mind of his own.

Never before had the thought occurred to him that Mike might disobey, that he might refuse. And if he did, what then? It was a rule of the outlaw pack that no man could leave it and live. It was a rule essential to their security. A few had tried, and their bodies now lay in Boot Hill. But Mike, his son? No, not Mike!

Within him, there was a deeper knowledge, an awareness that here his interests and those of the pack would divide. Even if he said no, they would say yes.

"Who would kill him, chief? Kerb Perrin? Rigger Molina? You?" Doc Sawyer shook his head slowly. "You *might* be able to do it, maybe one of the others, but I doubt it. You've created the man who may destroy you, chief, unless you join him."

Long after Doc Sawyer was gone, Ben Curry sat there staring out over the shadowed valley. He was getting old. For the first time he was beginning to doubt his rightness, beginning to wonder if he had not wronged Mike Bastian.

And what of Mike and Dru, his beloved, gray-eyed daughter? The girl with dash and spirit? But why not? Slowly he thought over Mike Bastian's life. Where was the boy wrong? Where was he unfitted for Dru? By the teachings given him by Curry's own suggestion? His own order? Or was there yet time?

Ben Curry heaved himself to his feet and began to pace the carpeted floor. He would have to decide. He would have to make up his mind, for a man's life and future lay in his hands, to make or break.

What if Dru wanted him anyway, outlaw or not? Ben Curry stopped and stared into the fireplace. If it had been Julie now, he might forbid it. But Dru? He chuckled. She would laugh at him. Dru had too much of his own nature, and she had a mind of her own.

Mike Bastian was restless the day after the excitement in Weaver. He rolled out of his bunk and walked out on the terrace. Only he and Doc Sawyer slept in the stone house where Ben Curry lived. Roundy was down in town with the rest of them, but tonight Mike wanted to walk, to think.

There had been a thrill of excitement in outtalking the sheriff, in facing down Fletcher, in flattening Corbus. And there had been more of it in facing Ducrow and Fernandez. Yet, was that what he wanted? Or did he want something more stable, more worthwhile? The something he might find with Drusilla Ragan?

Already he had won a place with the gang. He knew the story would be all over the outlaw camp now.

Walking slowly down the street of the settlement, he turned at right angles and drifted down a side road. He wanted to get away from things for a little while, to think things out. He turned again and stared back into the pines, and then he heard a voice coming from a nearby house. The words halted him.

". . . at Red Wall," Mike heard the ending.

Swiftly he glided to the house and flattened against the side. Kerb Perrin was speaking.

"It's a cinch, and we'll do it on our own without anybody's say-so. There's about two thousand cattle in the herd, and I've got a buyer for them. We can hit the place just about sunup. Right now, they have only four hands on the place, but about the first of next month they will start hiring. It's now or not at all."

"How many men will we take?" That was Ducrow speaking.

"A dozen. That will keep the divvy large enough, and they can swing it. Hell, that Ragan Ranch is easy. The boss won't hear about it until too late, and the chances are he will never guess it was us."

"I wouldn't want him to," Fernandez said.

"To hell with him!" Ducrow was irritated. "I'd like a crack at that Bastian again."

"Stick with me," Perrin said, "and I'll set him up for you. Curry is about to turn things over to him. Well, we'll beat him to it."

"You said there were girls?" Ducrow suggested.

"There's Curry's two girls and a couple of Mexican girls who work there. One older woman. I want one of those girls myself . . . the youngest of the Ragan sisters. What happens to the others is none of my business."

Mike Bastian's hand dropped to his gun, and his

lips tightened. The tone of Perrin's voice filled him with fury, and Ducrow was as bad as Perrin.

"What happens if Curry does find out?" Ducrow demanded.

"What would happen?" Perrin said fiercely. "I'll kill him like I've wanted to all these years. I've hated that man like I never hated anyone in my life."

"What about that Bastian?" Ducrow demanded.

Perrin laughed. "That's your problem. If you and Fernandez can't figure to handle him, then I don't know you."

"He knocked out Corbus, too," Ducrow said. "We might get him to throw in with us, if this crowd is all afraid of old Ben Curry."

"I ain't so sure about him my own self," said another voice, which Mike placed as belonging to an outlaw named Bayless. "He may not be so young any more, but he's hell on wheels with a gun."

"Forget him!" Perrin snapped. Then: "You three, and Clatt, Panelli, Monson, Kiefer and a few others, will go with us. All good men. There's a lot of dissatisfaction, anyway. Molina wants to raid the Mormons. They've a lot of rich stock, and there's no reason why we can't sell it south of the river and the other stock north of it. We can get rich."

V

Mike Bastian waited no longer, but eased away from the wall. He was tempted to wait for Perrin and brace him when he came out. His first thought was to go to Ben Curry, but he might betray his interest in Drusilla, and the time was not yet ripe for that. What would her father say if he found the foster son he had raised to be an outlaw was in love with his daughter?

It was foolish to think of it, yet he couldn't help it. There was time between now and the Twentieth for him to get back to Red Wall and see her.

A new thought occurred to him. Ben Curry would know the girls and their mother were there and would be going to see them. That would be his chance to learn of Ben's secret pass to the riverbank and how he crossed the Colorado.

Recalling other trips, Bastian knew the route must be a much quicker one than any he knew of, and was probably farther west and south, toward the cañon country. Already he was eager to see the girl again, and all he could think of was her trim figure, the laughter in her eyes, the soft curve of her lips.

There were other things to be considered. If there was as much unrest in the gang as Perrin said, things might be nearing a definite break. Certainly outlaws were not the men to stand hitched for long, and Ben Curry had commanded them for longer than anyone would believe. Their loyalty was due partly to the returns from their ventures under his guidance, and partly to fear of his far-reaching power. But he was growing old, and there were those among them who feared he was losing his grip.

Mike felt a sudden urge to saddle his horse and be gone, to get away from all this potential cruelty, the conniving and hatred that lay dormant here, or was seething and ready to explode. He could ride out now by the Kaibab trail through the forest, skirt the mountains, and find his own way through the cañon. It was a question whether he could escape, whether Ben Curry would let him go. To run now meant to abandon all hope of seeing Dru again, and Mike knew he could not do that.

Returning to his quarters in the big stone house, he stopped in front of a mirror. With deadly, flashing speed, he began to practice quick draws of his guns. Each night he did this twenty times as swiftly as his darting hands could move.

Finally he sat down on his bed thinking. Roundy first, and today Doc Sawyer. Each seemed to be hoping he would throw in the sponge and escape this outlaw life before it was too late. Doc said it was his life, but was it?

There was a light tap on the door. Gun in hand, he reached for the latch. Roundy stepped in. He glanced at the gun.

"Gettin' scary, Mike?" he queried. "Things are happenin'!"

"I know."

Mike went on to explain what he had overheard, and Roundy's face turned serious. "Mike, did you ever hear of Dave Lenaker?"

Bastian looked up. "You mean the Colorado gunman?"

"That's the one. He's headed this way. Ben Curry just got word that Lenaker's on his way to take over the Curry gang!"

"I thought he was one of Curry's ablest lieutenants?"

Roundy shrugged. "He was, Mike, but the word has gone out that the old man is losing his grip, and outlaws are quick to sense a thing like that. Lenaker never had any use for Perrin, and he's most likely afraid that Perrin will climb into the saddle. Dave Lenaker's a holy terror, too."

"Does Dad Curry know?" Mike said.

"Yeah. He's some wrought up, too," Roundy answered. "He was figurin' on bein' away for a few days, one of those trips he takes to Red Wall. Now he can't go."

Morning came cool and clear. Mike Bastian could feel disaster in the air, and he dressed hurriedly and headed for the bunkhouse. Few of the men were eating, and those few were silent. He knew they were all aware of impending change. He was finishing his coffee when Kerb Perrin came in.

Instantly Mike was on guard. Perrin walked with a strut, and his eyes were bright and confident. He glanced at Bastian, faintly amused, and then sat down at the table and began to eat.

Roundy came in, and then Doc Sawyer. Mike dallied over his coffee, and a few minutes later was rewarded by seeing Ducrow come in with Kiefer, followed in a few minutes by Rocky Clatt, Monson, and Panelli.

Suddenly, with the cup half to his mouth, Mike recalled with a shock that this was the group Perrin planned to use on his raid on the Ragan Ranch. That could mean the raid would come off today!

He looked up to see Roundy suddenly push back his chair and leave his breakfast unfinished. The old woodsman hurried outside and vanished.

Mike put down his own cup and got up. Then he stopped, motionless. The hard muzzle of a gun was prodding him in the back, and a voice was saying: "Don't move."

The voice was that of Fernandez, and Mike saw Perrin smiling.

"Sorry to surprise you, Bastian," Perrin said. "But with Lenaker on the road we had to move fast. By the time he gets here, I'll be in the saddle. Some of the boys wanted to kill you, but I figured you'd be a good talkin' point with the old man. He'd be a hard kernel to dig out of that stone shell of his without you. But with you for an argument, he'll come out all right."

"Have you gone crazy, Perrin? You can't get away with this."

"I am, though. You see, Rigger Molina left this morning with ten of his boys to work a little job they heard of. In fact, they are on their way to knock over the gold train."

"The gold train?" Bastian exclaimed. "Why, that was *my* job! He doesn't even know the plan made for it. Or the information I got."

Perrin smiled triumphantly. "I traded with him. I told him to give me a free hand here, and he could have the gold train. I neglected to tell him about the twelve guards riding with it, or the number with shotguns. In fact, I told him only five guards would be along. I think that will take care of Rigger for me." Perrin turned abruptly. "Take his guns and tie his hands behind his back, then shove him out into the street. I want the old man to see him."

"What about *him?*" Kiefer demanded, pointing a gun at Doc Sawyer.

"Leave him alone. We may need a doctor, and he knows where his bread is buttered."

Confused and angry, Mike Bastian was shoved out into the warm morning sun, then jerked around to face up the cañon toward the stone house.

Suddenly fierce triumph came over him. Perrin would have a time getting the old man out of that place. The sunlight was shining down the road from over the house, fully into their faces. The only approach to the house was up thirty steps of stone, overlooked by an upper window of the house. From that window and the doorway, the entire settlement could be commanded by an expert rifleman.

Ben Curry had thought of everything. The front and back doors of every building in the settlement could be commanded easily from his stronghold.

Perrin crouched behind a pile of sandbags hastily thrown up near the door of the store.

"Come on down, Curry!" he shouted. "Give yourself up or we'll kill Bastian!"

There was no answer from up the hill. Mike felt cold and sick in his stomach. Wind touched his hair and blew a strand down over his face. He stared up at the stone house and could see no movement, hear no response.

"Come on out!" Perrin roared again. "We know you're there! Come out or we'll kill your son!"

Still no reply.

"He don't hear you," Clatt said. "Maybe he's still asleep. Let's rush the place."

"You rush it," Kiefer said. "Let me watch!"

Despite his helplessness, Mike felt a sudden glow of satisfaction. Old Ben Curry was a wily fighter. He knew that once he showed himself or spoke, their threat would take force. It was useless to kill Bastian unless they knew Curry was watching them.

Perrin had been so sure Curry would come out rather than sacrifice Mike, and now they were not even sure he was hearing them! Nor, Mike knew suddenly, was anybody sure Ben would come out even if they did warn him Mike would be killed.

"Come on out!" Perrin roared. "Give yourself up and we'll give you and Bastian each a horse and a half mile start! Otherwise, you both die! We've got dynamite!"

Mike chuckled. Dynamite wasn't going to do them much good. There was no way to get close to that stone house, backed up against the mountain as it was.

"Perrin," he said, "you've played the fool. Curry doesn't care whether I live or die. He won't come out of there, and there's no way you can get at him. All he's got to do is sit tight and wait until Dave Lenaker gets here. He will make a deal with Dave then, and where will you be?"

"Shut up!" Perrin bellowed. But for the first time he seemed to be aware that his plan was not working. "He'll come out, all right."

"Let's open fire on the place," Ducrow suggested. "Or rush it like Clatt suggested."

"Hell!" Kiefer was disgusted. "Let's take what we can lay hands on and get out! There's two thousand head of cattle down in those bottoms.

Rigger's gone and Lenaker ain't here yet, so let's take what we can an' get out."

"Take pennies when there's millions up there in that stone house?" Perrin demanded. His face swelled in anger and the veins stood out on his forehead. "That strong room has gold in it! Stacks of money! I know it's there. With all that at hand, would you run off with a few cattle?"

Kiefer was silent but unconvinced.

Standing in the dusty street, Mike looked up at the stone house. All the loyalty and love he felt for the old man up there in that house came back with a rush. Whatever he was, good or bad, he owed to Ben Curry. Perhaps Curry had reared him for a life of crime, for outlawry, but to Ben Curry it was not a bad life. He lived like a feudal lord and had respect for no law he did not make himself.

Wrong he might be, but he had given the man that was Mike Bastian a start. Suddenly Mike knew that he could never have been an outlaw, that it was not in him to steal and rob and kill. But that did not mean he could be disloyal to the old man who had reared him and given him a home when he had none.

He was suddenly, fiercely proud of the old man up there alone. Like a cornered grizzly, he would fight to the death. He, Mike Bastian, might die here in the street, but he hoped old Ben Curry would stay in his stone shell and defeat them all.

Kerb Perrin was stumped. He had made his plan

quickly when he'd heard Dave Lenaker was on his way here, for he knew that, if Lenaker arrived, it might well turn into a bloody four-cornered fight. But with Molina out of the way, he might take over from Ben Curry before Lenaker arrived, and kill Lenaker and the men he brought with him in an ambush.

He had been sure that Ben Curry would reply, that he might give himself up or at least show himself, and Perrin had a sniper concealed to pick him off if he moved into the open. That he would get nothing but silence, he could not believe.

Mike Bastian stood alone in the center of the street. There was simply nothing he could do. At any moment Perrin might decide to have him killed where he stood. With his hands tied behind him, he was helpless. Mike wondered what had happened to Roundy? The old mountain man had risen suddenly from the table and vanished. Could he be in league with Perrin?

That was impossible. Roundy had always been Ben Curry's friend and had never liked anything about Kerb Perrin.

"All right," Perrin said suddenly, "we'll hold Bastian. He's still a good argument. Some men will stay here, and the rest of us will make that raid on the Ragan outfit. I've an idea that when we come back, Curry will be ready to talk business."

VI

Bastian was led back from the street and thrown into a room in the rear of the store. There his feet were tied and he was left in darkness.

His mind was in a turmoil. If Perrin's men hit the ranch now, they would take Drusilla and Juliana! He well knew how swiftly they would strike and how helpless any ordinary ranch would be against them. And here he was tied hand and foot, helpless to do anything!

He heaved his body around and fought the ropes that bound him, until sweat streamed from his body. Even then, with his wrists torn by his struggles against the rawhide thongs that made him fast, he did not stop. There was nothing to aid him—no nail, no sharp corner, nothing at all.

The room was built of thin boards nailed to two-by-fours. He rolled himself around until he could get his back against the boards, trying to remember where the nails were. Bracing himself as best he could, he pushed his back against the wall. He bumped against it until his back was sore. But with no effect.

Outside, all was still. Whether they had gone, he did not know. Yet, if Perrin had not gone on his raid, he would be soon leaving. However, if Mike could escape and find Curry's private route across the river, he might beat them to it.

He wondered where Doc Sawyer was. Perhaps he was afraid of what Perrin might do if he tried to help. Where was Roundy?

Just when he had all but given up, he had an idea—a solution so simple that he cursed himself for not thinking of it before. Mike rolled over and got up on his knees and reached back with his bound hands for his spurs. Fortunately he was wearing boots instead of the moccasins he wore in the woods. By wedging one spur against the other, he succeeded in holding the rowel almost immovable, and then he began to chafe the rawhide with the prongs of the rowel.

Desperately he sawed, until every muscle was crying for relief. As he stopped, he heard the rattle of horses' hoofs. They were just going! Then he had a fighting chance if he could get free and get his hands on a gun!

He knew he was making headway, for he could feel the notch he had already cut in the rawhide. Suddenly footsteps sounded outside. Fearful whoever was there would guess what he was doing, Mike rolled over on his side.

The door opened and Snake Fernandez came in, and in his hand he held a knife. His shoulder was bandaged crudely but tightly, and the knife was held in his left hand. He came in and closed the door.

Mike stared, horror mounting within him. Perrin was gone, and Snake Fernandez was moving toward him, smiling wickedly.

"You think you shoot Pablo Fernandez, eh?" the outlaw said, leering. "Now, we see who shoots. I am going to cut you to little pieces. I am going to cut you very slowly."

Bastian lay on his shoulder and stared at Fernandez. There was murder in the outlaw's eyes, and all the savagery in him was coming to the fore. The man stooped over him and pricked him with the knife. Clamping his jaws, Mike held himself tense.

Rage mounted in the man. He leaned closer. "You do not jump, eh? I make you jump."

He stabbed down hard with the knife, and Mike whipped over on his shoulder blades and kicked out wickedly with his bound feet. The movement caught the killer by surprise. Mike's feet hit him in the knees and knocked him rolling. With a lunge, Mike rolled over and jerked at the ropes that bound him.

Something snapped, and he jerked again. Like a cat the killer was on his feet now, circling warily. Desperately Mike pulled at the ropes, turning on his shoulders to keep his feet toward Fernandez. Suddenly he rolled over and hurled himself at the Mexican's legs, but Fernandez jerked back and stabbed.

Mike felt a sliver of pain run along his arms, and then he rolled to his feet and jerked wildly at the thongs. His hands came loose suddenly and he hurled himself at Fernandez's legs, grabbing one ankle.

Fernandez came down hard, and Bastian jerked at the leg, and then scrambled to get at him. One hand grasped the man's wrist, the other his throat. With all the power that was in him, Mike shut down on both hands.

Fernandez fought like an injured wildcat, but Mike's strength was too great. Gripping the throat with his left hand, Mike slammed the Mexican's head against the floor again and again, his throttling grip freezing tighter and tighter.

The outlaw's face went dark with blood, and his struggles grew weaker. Mike let go of his throat hold suddenly and slugged him three times on the chin with his fist.

Jerking the knife from the unconscious man's hand, Mike slashed at the thongs that bound his ankles. He got to his feet shakily. Glancing down at the sprawled-out Fernandez, he hesitated. The man was not wearing a gun, but must have had one. It could be outside the door. Easing to the door, Mike opened it a crack.

The street was deserted as far as he could see. His hands felt awkward from their long constraint, and he worked his fingers to loosen them up. There was no gun in sight, so he pushed the door wider. Fernandez's gun belts hung over the chair on the end of the porch.

He had taken two steps toward them when a man stepped out of the bunkhouse. The fellow had a toothpick lifted to his lips, but when he saw Mike

Bastian, he let out a yelp of surprise and went for his gun.

It was scarcely fifteen paces and Mike threw the knife underhanded, pitching it point first off the palm of his hand. It flashed in the sun as the fellow's gun came up. Then Mike could see the haft protruding from the man's middle section.

The fellow screamed and, dropping the gun, clutched at the knife hilt in an agony of fear. His breath came in horrid gasps that Mike could hear as he grabbed Fernandez's guns and belted them on. Then he lunged for the mess hall, where his own guns had been taken from him. Shoving open the door, he sprang inside, gun in hand.

Then he froze. Doc Sawyer was standing there smiling, and Doc had a shotgun on four of Perrin's men. He looked up with relief.

"I was hoping you would escape," he said. "I didn't want to kill these men and didn't know how to go about tying them up by myself."

Mike caught up his own guns, removed Fernandez's gun belts, and strapped on his own. Then he shoved the outlaw's guns inside the waistband of his pants.

"Down on the floor," he ordered. "I'll tie them, and fast."

It was the work of only a few minutes to have the four outlaws bound hand and foot. He gathered up their guns. "Where's Roundy?" he asked.

"I haven't seen him since he left here," Doc said. "I've been wondering."

"Let's go up to the house. We'll get Ben Curry, and then we'll have things under control in a hurry."

Together, they went out the back door and walked swiftly down the line of buildings. Mike took off his hat and sailed it into the brush, knowing he could be seen from the stone house and hoping that Ben Curry would recognize him. Sawyer was excited, but trying to appear calm. He had been a gambler and, while handy with guns, was not a man accustomed to violence. Always before, he had been a bystander rather than an active participant.

Side-by-side, gambling against a shot from someone below, they went up the stone stairs.

There was no sound from within the house. They walked into the wide living room and glanced around. There was no sign of anyone. Then Mike saw a broken box of rifle shells.

"He's been around here," he said. Then he looked up and shouted: "Dad!"

A muffled cry reached them, and Mike was out of the room and up another staircase. He entered the room at the top, and then froze in his tracks. Sawyer was behind him now.

This was the fortress room, a heavy-walled stone room that had water trickling from a spring in the wall of the cliff and running down a stone trough and out through a pipe. There was food stored here, and plenty of ammunition.

The door was heavy and could be locked and barred from within. The walls of this room were all of four feet thick, and nothing short of dynamite could have blasted a way in.

This was Ben Curry's last resort, and he was here now. But he was sprawled on the floor, his face contorted with pain.

"Broke my leg," he panted. "Too heavy. Tried to move too . . . fast. Slipped on the steps, dragged myself up here." He looked up at Mike. "Good for you, Son! I was afraid they had killed you. You got away by yourself?"

"Yes, Dad."

Sawyer had dropped to his knees, and now he looked up.

"This is a bad break, Mike," he said. "He won't be able to move."

"Get me on a bed where I can see out of that window." Ben Curry's strength seemed to flow back with his son's presence. "I'll stand them off. You and me, Mike, we can do it!"

"Dad," Mike said. "I can't stay. I've got to go."

Ben Curry's face went gray with shock, then slowly the blood flowed back into it. Bastian dropped down beside him.

"Dad, I know where Perrin's going. He's gone to make a raid on the Ragan Ranch. He wants the cattle and the women."

The old man lunged so mightily that Sawyer cried out and tried to push him back. Before he could speak, Mike said: "Dad, you must tell me about the secret crossing of the Colorado that you know. I must beat them to the ranch."

Ben Curry's expression changed to one of vast relief and then quick calculation. He nodded. "You could do it, but it'll take tall riding." Quickly he outlined the route, and then added: "Now, listen! At the river there's an old Navajo. He keeps some horses for me, and he has six of the finest animals ever bred. You cross that river and get a horse from him. He knows about you."

Mike got up. "Make him comfortable, Doc. Do all you can."

Sawyer stared at Mike. "What about Dave Lenaker? He'll kill us all!"

"I'll take care of Lenaker!" Curry flared. "I'm not dead by a danged sight. I'll show that renegade where he heads in. The moment he comes up that street, I'm going to kill him." He looked at Mike again. "Son, maybe I've done wrong to raise you like I have, but if you kill Kerb Perrin or Lenaker, you would be doing the West a favor. If I don't get Dave Lenaker, you may have to. So remember this, *watch his left hand!*"

Mike ran down the steps and stopped in his room to grab his .44 Winchester. It was the work of a minute to throw a saddle on a horse, and then he hit the trail. Ben Curry and Doc Sawyer could, if necessary, last for days in the fortress-like room—unless, somehow, dynamite was pitched into the window. He would have to get to the Ragan Ranch and then get back here as soon as possible.

Mike Bastian left the stable and wheeled the gray he was riding into the long, winding trail through the stands of ponderosa and fir. The horse was in fine fettle and ready for the trail, and he let it out. His mind was leaping over the trail, turning each bend, trying to see how it must lay.

This was all new country to him, for he was heading southwest now into the wild, unknown region toward the great cañons of the Colorado, a region he had never traversed and, except for old Ben Curry, was perhaps never crossed by any except Indians.

How hard the trail would be on the horse, Mike could not guess, but he knew he must ride fast and keep going. His route was the shorter, but Kerb Perrin had a lead on him and would be hurrying to make his strike and return.

Patches of snow still hid themselves around the roots of the brush and in the hollows under the end of some giant deadfall. The air was crisp and chill, but growing warmer, and by afternoon it would be hot in the sunlight. The wind of riding whipped his black hair. He ran the horse down a long path bedded deep with pine needles, and then turned at a blazed tree and went out across the arid top of a plateau.

This was the strange land he loved, the fiery, heat-blasted land of the sun. Riding along the crest of a long ridge, he looked out over a long valley dotted with mesquite and sagebrush. Black dots of cattle grazing offered the only life beyond the lonely, lazy swing of a high-soaring buzzard.

He saw the white rock he had been told to look for and turned the free-running horse into a cleft that led downward. They moved slowly here, for it was a steep slide down the side of the mesa and out on the long roll of the hill above the valley.

Time and time again Mike's hand patted his guns, as if to reassure himself they were there. His thoughts leaped ahead, trying to foresee what would happen. Would he arrive only to find the buildings burned and the girls gone?

He knew only that he must get there first, that he must face them, and that at all costs he must kill Kerb Perrin and Ducrow. Without them, the others might run, might not choose to fight it out. Mike had an idea that without Perrin, they would scatter to the four winds.

Swinging along the hillside, he took a trail that led again to a plateau top and ran off through the sage, heading for the smoky-blue distance of the cañon.

VII

Mike's mind lost track of time and distance, leaping ahead to the river and the crossing, and beyond it to Ragan's V Bar Ranch. Down steep trails through the great, broken cliffs heaped high with the piled-up stone of ages, and down through the wild, weird jumble of boulders, and across the flat top lands that smelled of sage and piñon, he kept the horse moving.

Then he was once more in the forests of the Kaibab. The dark pines closed around him, and he rode on in the vast stillness of virgin timber, the miles falling behind, the trail growing dim before him.

Then suddenly the forest split aside and he was on the rim of the cañon—an awful blue immensity yawning before him that made him draw the gray to a halt in gasping wonder. Far out over that vast, misty blue rose islands of red sandstone, islands that were laced and crossed by bands of purple and yellow. The sunset was gleaming on the vast plateaus and buttes and peaks with a ruddy glow, fading into opaqueness in the deeper cañon.

The gray was beaten and weary now. Mike turned the horse toward a break in the plateau and rode down it, giving the animal its head. They came out upon a narrow trail that hung above a vast gorge, its bottom lost in the darkness of gathering dusk. The gray stumbled on, seeming to know its day was almost done.

Dozing in the saddle, almost two hours later Mike Bastian felt the horse come to a halt. He jerked his head up and opened his eyes. He could feel the dampness of a deep cañon and could hear the thundering roar of the mighty river as it charged through the rock-walled slit. In front of him was a square of light.

"Halloo, the house!" he called.

He swung down as the door opened.

"Who's there?" a voice cried out.

"Mike Bastian!" he said, moving toward the house with long, swinging strides. "For Ben Curry!"

The man backed into the house. He was an ancient Navajo, but his eyes were keen and sharp.

"I want a horse," Mike said.

"You can't cross the river tonight." The Navajo spoke English well. "It is impossible."

"There'll be a moon later," Mike answered. "When it comes up, I'm going across."

The Indian looked at him, and then shrugged.

"Eat," he said. "You'll need it."

"There are horses?"

"Horses?" The Navajo chuckled. "The best a man ever saw. Do you suppose Ben Curry would have horses here that were not the best? But they are on the other side of the stream, and safe enough. My brother is with them."

Mike fell into a seat. "Take care of my horse, will you? I've most killed him."

When the Indian was gone, Mike slumped over on the table, burying his head in his arms. In a moment he was asleep, dreaming wild dreams of a mad race over a strange misty-blue land with great crimson islands, riding a splendid black horse and carrying a girl in his arms. He awakened with a start. The old Indian was sitting by the fireplace, and he looked up.

"You'd better eat," he said. "The moon is rising."

They went out together, walking down the path to the water's edge. As the moon shone down into the cañon, Mike stared at the tumbling stream in consternation. Nothing living could swim in that water! It would be impossible.

"How do you cross?" he demanded. "No horse could swim that. And a boat wouldn't get fifty feet before it would be dashed to pieces."

The Indian chuckled. "That isn't the way we cross it. You are right in saying no boat could cross here, for there is no landing over there, and the cañon is so narrow that the water piles up back of the narrows and comes down with a great rush."

Mike looked at him again. "You talk like an educated man," he said. "I don't understand."

The Navajo shrugged. "I was for ten years with a missionary, and after I traveled with him as an interpreter he took me back to the States, where I stayed with him for two years. Then I lived in Sante Fé."

He was leading the way up a steep path that skirted the cliff but was wide enough to walk comfortably. Opposite them, the rock wall of the cañon lifted and the waters of the tumbling river roared down through the narrow chasm.

"Ben Curry does things well, as you shall see," the guide said. "It took him two years of effort to get this bridge built."

Mike stared. "Across there?"

"Yes. A bridge for a man with courage. It is a rope bridge, made fast to iron rings sunk in the rock."

Mike Bastian walked on the rocky ledge at the edge of the trail and looked out across the gorge. In the pale moonlight he could see two slim threads trailing across the cañon high above the tumbling water. Just two ropes, and one of them four feet above the other.

"You mean," he said, "that Ben Curry crossed on *that?*"

"He did. I have seen him cross that bridge a dozen times, at least."

"Have you crossed it?"

The Navajo shrugged. "Why should I? The other side is the same as this, is it not? There is nothing over there that I want."

Mike looked at the slender strands, and then he took hold of the upper rope and tentatively put a foot on the lower one. Slowly, carefully he eased out above the raging waters.

One slip and he would be gone, for no man could hope to live in those angry flood waters. He slid his foot along, then the other, advancing his handholds as he moved. Little by little, he worked his way across the cañon.

He was trembling when he got his feet in the rocky cavern on the opposite side and so relieved to be safely across that he scarcely was aware of the old Indian who sat there awaiting him.

The Navajo got up and without a word started down the trail. He quickly led Mike to a cabin built in the opening of a dry, branch cañon, and tethered before the door of the cabin was a huge bay stallion.

Waving at the Indian, Mike swung into the saddle, and the bay turned, taking to the trail as if eager to be off.

Would Perrin travel at night? Mike doubted it, but it was possible, so he kept moving himself. The trail led steadily upward, winding finally out of the cañon to the plateau.

The bay stallion seemed to know the trail; it was probable that Curry had used this horse himself. It was a splendid animal, big and very fast. Letting the horse have his head, Mike felt the animal gather his legs under him. Then he broke into a long, swinging lope that literally ate up the ground. How long the horse could hold that speed he did not know, but it was a good start.

It was at least a ten-hour ride to the Ragan V Bar Ranch.

The country was rugged and wild. Several times, startled deer broke and ran before him, and there were many rabbits. Dawn was breaking faintly in the east now, and shortly after daybreak he stopped near a pool of melted snow water and made coffee. Then he remounted the rested stallion and raced on.

Drusilla Ragan brushed her hair thoughtfully, and then pinned it up. Outside, she could hear her mother moving about and the Mexican girls who helped around the house whenever they were visiting. Julie was up, she knew, and had been up for hours. She was outside, talking to that blond cowhand from New Mexico, the one Voyle Ragan had hired to break horses.

Suddenly she heard Julie's footsteps, and then the door opened.

"Aren't you ready yet?" Julie asked. "I'm famished!"

"I'll be along in a minute." Then as Julie turned to go: "What did you think of him, Julie . . . that cowboy who got the buckboard for us? Wasn't he the handsomest thing?"

"Oh, you mean that Mike Bastian?" Julie said. "I was wondering why you were mooning around in here. Usually you're the first one up. Yes, I expect he is good-looking. But did you see the way he looked when you mentioned Uncle Voyle? He acted so strange."

"I wonder if Uncle Voyle knows anything about him? Let's ask!"

"You ask," Julie replied, laughing. "He's *your* problem!"

Voyle Ragan was a tall man, but lean and without Ben Curry's weight. He was already seated at the table when they came in, and Dru was no sooner in her seat than she put her question. Voyle's face became a mask.

"Mike Bastian?" he said thoughtfully. "I don't know. Where'd you meet him?"

The girls explained, and he nodded.

"In Weaver?" Voyle Ragan knew about the gold train, and his eyes narrowed. "I think I know who he is, but I never saw him that I heard of. You probably won't see him again, because most of those riders from up in the strip stay there most of time. They are a wild bunch."

"On the way down here," Julie said, "the man who drove was telling us that outlaws live up there."

"Could be. It's wild enough." Voyle Ragan lifted his head, listening. For a moment he had believed he heard horses. But it was too soon for Ben to be coming. If anyone else came, he would have to get rid of them, and quickly.

He heard the sound again, and then he saw the cavalcade of horsemen riding into the yard. Voyle came to his feet abruptly.

"Stay here!" he snapped.

His immediate thought was of a posse, and then he saw Kerb Perrin. He had seen Perrin many times, although Perrin had never met him. Slowly he moved up to the door, uncertain of his course. These were Ben's men, but Ben had always told him that none of them was aware that he owned this ranch or that Voyle was his brother.

"Howdy!" Voyle said. "What can I do for you?"

Kerb Perrin swung down from his horse. Behind him Monson, Ducrow, and Kiefer were getting down.

"You can make as little trouble as you know how," Perrin said, his eyes gleaming. "All you got to do is stay out of the way. Where's the girls? We want them, and we want your cattle."

"What is this?" Voyle demanded. He wasn't wearing a gun; it was hanging from a clothestree in the next room. "You men can't get away with anything here!"

Perrin's face was ugly as he strode toward the door. "That's what *you* think," he sneered.

The tall old man blocked his way, and Perrin shoved him aside. Perrin had seen the startled faces of the girls inside and knew the men behind him were spreading out.

Ragan swung suddenly, and his fist struck Perrin in the mouth. The gunman staggered, and his face went white with fury.

A Mexican started from the corral toward the house, and Ducrow wheeled, firing from the hip. The man cried out and sprawled over on the hard-packed earth, moaning out his agony.

Perrin had drawn back slowly, his face ugly with rage, a slow trickling of blood from his lips. "For that, I'll kill you!" he snarled at Ragan.

"Not yet, Perrin!"

The voice had a cold ring of challenge, and Kerb Perrin went numb with shock. He turned slowly, to see Mike Bastian standing at the corner of the corral.

VIII

Kerb Perrin was profoundly shocked. He had left Bastian a prisoner at Toadstool Cañon. Since he was free now, it could mean that Ben Curry was back in the saddle. It could mean a lot of things. An idea came with startling clarity to him. He had to kill Mike Bastian, and kill him now!

"You men have made fools of yourselves!" Bastian's voice was harsh. He stood there in his gray buckskins, his feet a little apart, his black hair rippled by the wind. "Ben Curry's not through! And this place is under his protection. He sent me to stop you, and stop you I shall! Now, any of you who don't want to fight Ben Curry, get out while the getting is good!"

"Stay where you are!" Perrin snapped. "I'll settle with you, Bastian . . . right now!"

His hand darted down in the sweeping, lightning-fast draw for which he was noted. His lips curled in sneering contempt. Yet, as his gun lifted, he saw flame blossom from a gun in Bastian's hand, and a hard object slugged him. Perplexed and disturbed, he took a step backward. Whatever had hit him had knocked his gun out of line. He turned it toward Bastian again. The gun in Mike's hand blasted a second time, and a third.

Perrin could not seem to get his own gun leveled. His mind wouldn't function right, and he felt a strangeness in his stomach, his legs—suddenly he was on his knees. He tried to get up and saw a dark pool forming near his knees. He must have slipped, he must have—that was blood.

It was his blood!

From far off he heard shouts, then a scream, then the pound of horses' hoofs. Then the thunder of those hoofs seemed to sweep through his brain and he was lying face down in the dirt. And then he knew. Mike Bastian had beaten him to the draw. Mike Bastian had shot him three times. Mike Bastian had killed him!

He started to scream a protest—and then he just lay there on his face, his cheek against the bloody ground, his mouth half open.

Kerb Perrin was dead.

In the instant that Perrin had reached for his gun, Ducrow had suddenly cut and run toward the corner of the house. Kiefer, seeing his leader gunned down, then made a wild grab for his own weapon. The old man in the doorway killed him with a hastily caught up rifle.

The others broke for their horses. Mike rushed after them and got off one more shot as they raced out of the yard. It was then he heard the scream, and whirled.

Ducrow had acted with suddenness. He had come to the ranch for women, and women he intended to have. Even as Bastian was killing Perrin, he had rushed for the house. Darting around the corner where two saddle horses were waiting, he was just in time to see Juliana, horrified at the killing, run back into her bedroom. The bedroom window opened beside Ducrow, and the outlaw reached through and grabbed her.

Julie went numb with horror. Ducrow threw her across Perrin's saddle, and with a pigging string, which he always carried from his days as a cowhand, he jerked her ankles together under the horse's belly.

Instantly he was astride the other horse. Julie screamed then. Wheeling, he struck her across the mouth with a backhand blow. He caught up the bridle of her horse and drove in spurs to his own mount, and they went out of the ranch yard at a dead run.

Mike hesitated only an instant when he heard Julie scream, and then ran for the corner of the house. By the time he rounded the corner, gun in hand, the two horses were streaking into the piñons. In the dust, he could only catch a glimpse of the riders. He turned and walked back.

That had been a woman's scream, but Dru was in the doorway and he had seen her. Only then did he recall Julie. He sprinted for the doorway.

"Where's Julie?" he shouted to Drusilla. "Look through the house!"

He glanced around quickly. Kerb Perrin, mouth agape, lay dead on the hard earth of the ranch yard. Kiefer lay near the body of the Mexican Ducrow had killed. The whole raid had been a matter of no more than two or three minutes.

Voyle Ragan dashed from the house. "Julie's gone!" he yelled hoarsely. "I'll get a horse!"

Bastian caught his arm. His own dark face was tense and his eyes wide.

"You'll stay here!" he said harshly. "Take care of the women and the ranch. I'll go after Julie."

Dru ran from the house. "She's gone, Mike, she's gone! They have her!"

Mike walked rapidly to his horse, thumbing shells into his gun. Dru Ragan started to mount another horse. "You go back to the house," he ordered.

Dru's chin came up. In that moment she reminded him of Ben Curry.

"She's my sister!" Dru cried. "When we find her, she may need a woman's care!"

"All right," Mike said, "but you'll have to do some riding."

He wheeled the big bay around. The horse Dru had mounted was one of Ben Curry's beautiful horses, bred not only for speed but for staying power.

Mike's mind leaped ahead. Would Ducrow get back with the rest of them? Would he join Monson and Clatt? If he did, it was going to be a problem. Ducrow was a handy man with a six-gun, and tackling the three of them, or more if they were all together, would be nothing less than suicide.

He held the bay horse's pace down. He had taken a swift glance at the hoof marks of the horses he was trailing and knew them both.

Would Ducrow head back for Toadstool Cañon? Bastian considered that as he rode, and decided he would not. Ducrow did not know that Julie was Ben Curry's daughter. But from what Mike had said, Ducrow had cause to believe that Ben was back in the saddle again. And men who went off on rebel raids were not lightly handled by Curry. Besides, he would want, if possible, to keep the girl for himself.

Mike had been taught by Roundy that there was more to trailing a man than following his tracks, for you trailed him down the devious paths of the mind as well. He tried to put himself in Ducrow's place.

The man could not have much food, yet on his many outlaw forays he must have learned the country and would know where there was water. Also, there were many ranch hang-outs of the outlaws that Ducrow would know. He would probably go to one of them. Remembering the maps that Ben Curry had shown him and made him study, Mike knew the locations of all those places.

The trail turned suddenly off through the chaparral, and Mike turned to follow. Drusilla had said nothing since they started. Once he glanced at her. Even now, with her face dusty and tear-streaked, she was lovely. Her eyes were fastened on the trail, and he noted with a little thrill of satisfaction that she had brought her rifle along.

Dru certainly was her father's daughter, and a fit companion for any man.

Bastian turned his attention back to the trail. Despite the small lead he had, Ducrow had vanished. That taught Mike something of the nature of the man he was tracing; his years of outlawry had taught him how to disappear when need be. The method was simple. Turning off into the thicker desert growth, he had ridden down into a sandy wash.

Here, because of the deep sand and the tracks of horses and cattle, tracking was a problem and it took Mike several minutes to decide whether Ducrow had gone up or down the wash. Then he caught a hoof print and they were off, winding up the sandy wash. Yet Mike knew they would not be in that sand for long. Ducrow would wish to save his horses' strength.

True enough, the trail soon turned out. From then on, it was a nightmare. Ducrow ran off in a straightaway, and then turned at right angles, weaving about in the sandy desert. Several times he had stopped to brush out portions of his trail, but Roundy had not spent years training Mike Bastian in vain. He hung to the trail like a bloodhound.

Dru, riding behind him, saw him get off and walk, saw him pick up sign where she could see nothing.

Hours passed, and the day slowly drew toward an end. Dru, her face pale, realized night would come before they found her sister. She was about to speak, when Mike looked at her.

"You wanted to come," he said, "so you'll have to take the consequences. I'm not stopping because of darkness."

"How can you trail them?"

"I can't." He shrugged. "But I think I know where they are going. We'll take a chance."

Darkness closed around them. Mike's shirt stuck to his body with sweat, and a chill wind off the higher plateaus blew down through the trees. He rode on, his face grim and his body weary with long hours in the saddle. The big bay kept on, seemingly unhurt by the long hours of riding. Time and again he patted the big horse, and Dru could hear him talking to it in a low voice. Suddenly at the edge of a clearing, he reined in.

"Dru," he said, "there's a ranch ahead. It's an outlaw hang-out. There may be one or more men there. Ducrow may be there. I am going up to find out."

"I'll come, too," the girl said impulsively.

"You'll stay here." His voice was flat. "When I whistle, then you come. Bring my horse along."

He swung down and, slipping off his boots, pulled on his moccasins. Then he went forward into the darkness. Alone, she watched him vanish toward the dark bulk of the buildings. Suddenly a light came on—too soon for him to have arrived.

Mike weaved his way through sage and mesquite to the corral and worked his way along the bars. Horses were there, but it was too dark to make them out. One of them stood near, and he put his hand through the bars, touching the horse's flank. It was damp with sweat.

His face tightened.

The horse stepped away, snorting. As if waiting for just that sound, a light went on in the house; a lamp had been lighted. By that time Mike was at the side of the house, flattened against the wall, peering in.

He saw a heavy, square-faced man with a pistol in his hand. The man put the gun under a towel on the table, and then began pacing around the room, waiting. Mike smiled grimly, walked around the house, and stepped up on the porch. In his moccasins, he made no sound. He opened the door suddenly and stepped into the room.

IX

Obviously the man had been waiting for the sound of boots or horses, or the *jingle* of spurs. Even a knock. Mike Bastian's sudden appearance startled him, and he straightened up from the table, his hand near the towel that covered the gun.

Bastian closed the door behind him. The man stared at the black-haired young man who faced him, stared with puckered brow. This man didn't look like a sheriff to him. Not those tied-down guns or that gray buckskin stained with travel, and no hat.

"You're Walt Sutton," Mike snapped. "Get your hands off that table before I blow you wide open. Get 'em off!"

He drew his gun and jammed the muzzle into Sutton's stomach with such force that it doubled the man up.

Then he swept the towel from the gun on the table.

"You fool!" he said sharply. "If you'd tried that, I'd have killed you!"

Sutton staggered back, his face gray. He had never even seen Mike's hand move.

"Who are you?" he gasped, struggling to get his wind back.

"I'm Mike Bastian, Ben Curry's foster son. He owns this ranch. He set you up here and gave you stock to get started with. Now you double-cross him! Where's Ducrow?"

Sutton swallowed. "I ain't seen him!" he protested.

"You're a liar, Sutton. His horses are out in that corral. I could pistol-whip you, but I'm not going to. You're going to tell me where he is, and now . . . or I'm going to start shooting!"

Walt Sutton was unhappy. He knew Ducrow as one of Ben Curry's men who had come here before for fresh horses. He had never seen this man who called himself Mike Bastian, yet, so far as he knew, no one but Curry himself had ever known the true facts about his ranch. If this man was lying, how could he know?

"Listen, mister," he protested, "I don't want no trouble . . . least of all with old Ben. He did set me up here. Sure, I seen Ducrow, but he told me the law was after him."

"Do I look like the law?" Mike snapped. "He's kidnapped the daughter of a friend of Curry's, niece of Voyle Ragan. I've got to find him."

123

"Kidnapped Voyle's niece? Gosh, mister, I wondered why he wanted two saddle horses."

Mike whistled sharply. "Where'd he go?" he demanded then.

"Damned if I know," Sutton answered. "He come in here maybe an hour ago, wanted two saddle horses and a pack horse loaded with grub. He took two canteens then and lit out."

Drusilla appeared now in the doorway, and Walt Sutton's eyes went to her.

"I know you," he said. "You're one of Voyle Ragan's nieces."

"She is," Mike said. "Ducrow kidnapped the other one. I'm going to find him. Get us some grub, but fast!"

Mike paced restlessly while Sutton filled a pack and strapped it behind the saddle of one of the fresh horses he furnished them. The horses were some of those left at the ranch by Ben Curry's orders and were good.

"No pack horses," Mike had said. "We're traveling fast." Now, he turned to Sutton again. "You got any idea where Ducrow might be going?"

"Well"—Sutton licked his lips—"he'd kill me if he knowed I said anything, but he did say something about Peach Meadow Cañon."

"Peach Meadow?" Bastian stared at Sutton. The cañon was almost a legend in the Coconino country. "What did he ask you?"

"If I knowed the trail in there, an' if it was passable."

"What did you say?"

Sutton shrugged. "Well, I've heard tell of that there cañon ever since I been in this country, an' ain't seen no part of it. I've looked, all right. Who wouldn't look, if all they say is true?"

When they were about to mount their horses, Mike turned to the girl and put his hand on her arm.

"Dru," he said, "it's going to be rough, so if you want to go back, say so."

"I wouldn't think of it," she said firmly.

"Well, I won't say I'm sorry, because I'm not. I'll sure like having you beside me. In fact"—he hesitated, and then went on—"it will be nice having you."

That was not what he had started to say, and Dru knew it. She looked at Mike for a moment, her eyes soft. He was tired now, and she could see how drawn his face was. She knew only a little of the ride he had made to reach them before Perrin's outlaws came.

When they were in the saddle, Mike explained a little of what he had in mind. "I doubt Ducrow will stop for anything now," he said. "There isn't a good hiding place within miles, so he'll head right for the cañon country. He may actually know something about Peach Meadow Cañon. If he does, he knows a perfect hideaway. Outlaws often stumble across places in their getaways that a man couldn't find if he looked for it in years."

"What is Peach Meadow Cañon?" Dru asked.

"It's supposed to be over near the river in one of the deep cañons that branch off from the Colorado. According to the story, a fellow found the place years ago, but the Spanish had been there before him, and the Indians before them. There are said to be old Indian ruins in the place, but no way to get into it from the plateau. The Indians found a way through some caves in the Coconino sandstone, and the Spanish are supposed to have reached it by boat.

"Anyway," he continued, "this prospector who found it said the climate was tropical, or almost. That it was in a branch cañon, that there was fresh water and a nice meadow. Somebody had planted some fruit trees, and, when he went back, he took a lot of peach pits and was supposed to have planted an orchard.

"Nobody ever saw him or it again," Mike went on, "so the place exists only on his say-so. The Indians alive now swear they never heard of it. Ducrow might be trying to throw us off, or he might honestly know something."

For several miles the trail was a simple thing. They were riding down the floor of a high-walled cañon from which there was no escape. Nevertheless, from time to time Bastian stopped and examined the sandy floor with matches. Always the tracks were there and going straight down the cañon.

This was new country to Mike. He knew the altitude was gradually lessening and believed they would soon emerge on the desert plateau that ran toward the cañon and finally lost itself on the edge of the pine forest.

When they had traveled about seven miles, the cañon ended abruptly and they emerged in a long valley. Mike reined in and swung down.

"Like it or not," he said, "here's where we stop. We can't have a fire, because from here it could be seen for miles. We don't want Ducrow to believe we stopped."

Mike spread his poncho on the sand and handed Dru a blanket. She was feeling the chill and gathered it closely around her.

"Aren't you cold?" she said suddenly. "If we sat close together, we could share the blanket."

He hesitated, and then sat down alongside her and pulled the blanket across his shoulders, grateful for the warmth. Leaning back against the rock, warmed by their proximity and the blanket, they dozed a little.

Mike had loosened the girths and ground-hitched the horses. He wasn't worried about them straying off.

When the sky was just faintly gray, he opened his eyes. Dru's head was on his shoulder and she was sleeping. He could feel the rise and fall of her breathing against his body. He glanced down at her face, amazed that this could happen to him—that he, Mike Bastian, foster son of an outlaw, could be sitting alone in the desert, with this girl sleeping on his shoulder.

Some movement of his must have awakened her, for her breath caught, and then she looked up. He could see the sleepy smile in her eyes and on her mouth.

"I was tired." She whispered the words and made no effort to move her head from his shoulder. "You've nice shoulders," she said. "If we were riding anywhere else, I'd not want to move at all."

"Nor I." He glanced at the stars. "We'd better get up. I think we can chance a very small fire and a quick cup of coffee."

While he was breaking dried mesquite and greasewood, Dru got the pack open and dug out the coffee and some bread. There was no time for anything else.

The fire made but little light, shielded by the rocks and kept very small, and there was less glow now because of the grayness of the sky. They ate quickly.

When they were in the saddle again, he turned down the trail left by the two saddle horses and the pack horse he was following. Sign was dim, but could be followed without dismounting. Dawn

128

broke, and the sky turned red and gold, then blue. The sun lifted and began to take some of the chill from their muscles.

The trail crossed the valley, skirting an alkali lake, and then dipped into the rocky wilderness that preceded the pine forest. He could find no signs of a camp. Julie, who lacked the fire and also the strength of Dru, must be almost dead with weariness, for Ducrow was not stopping. Certainly the man had more than a possible destination before him. In fact, the farther they rode, the more confident Mike was that the outlaw knew exactly where he was headed.

The pines closed around them, and the trail became more difficult to follow. It was slow going, and much of it Mike Bastian walked. Suddenly he stopped, scowling.

The trail, faint as it had been, had vanished into thin air!

"Stay where you are," he told Dru. "I've got to look around a bit."

Mike studied the ground carefully. Then he walked back to the last tracks he had seen. Their own tracks did not cover them, as he had avoided riding over them in case he needed to examine the hoof prints once more.

Slowly Mike paced back and forth over the pine needles. Then he stopped and studied the surrounding timber very carefully. It seemed to be absolutely uniform in appearance. Avoiding the trail ahead, he left the girl and circled into the woods, describing a slow circle around the horses.

There were no tracks.

He stopped, his brow furrowed. It was impossible to lose them after following so far—yet they were gone, and they had left no trail. He walked back to the horses again, and Dru stared at him, her eyes wide.

"Wait a minute," he said as she began to speak. "I want to think."

He studied, inch by inch, the woods on his left, the trail ahead, and then the trail on his right. Nothing offered a clue. The tracks of three horses had simply vanished as though the animals and their riders had been swallowed into space.

On the left the pines stood thick, and back inside the woods the brush was so dense as to allow no means of passing through it. That was out, then. He had studied that brush and had walked through those woods, and, if a horseman did turn that way there would be no place to go.

The trail ahead was trackless, so it had to be on the right. Mike turned and walked again to the woods on his right. He inched over the ground, yet there was nothing, no track, no indication that anything heavier than a rabbit had passed that way. It was impossible, yet it had happened.

"Could they have backtracked?" Dru asked suddenly. "Over their same trail?"

Mike shook his head. "There were no tracks," he

said, "but those going ahead, I think. . . ." He stopped dead still, and then swore. "I'm a fool! A darned fool!" He grinned at her. "Lend me your hat."

Puzzled, she removed her sombrero and handed it to him. He turned and, using the hat for a fan, began to wave it over the ground to let the wind disturb the surface needles. Patiently he worked over the area around the last tracks seen, and then to the woods on both sides of the trail. Suddenly he stopped.

"Got it," he said. "Here they are."

Dru ran to him. He pointed to a track, then several more.

"Ducrow was smart," Mike explained. "He turned at right angles and rode across the open space, and then turned back down the way he had come, riding over on the far side. Then he dismounted and, coming back, gathered pine needles from somewhere back in the brush and came along here, pressing the earth down and scattering the needles to make it seem there had been no tracks at all."

Mounting again, they started back, and from time to time he dismounted to examine the trail. Suddenly the tracks turned off into thick woods. Leading their horses, they followed.

"Move as quietly as you can," Mike said softly. "We may be close now. Or he may wait and try to ambush us."

"You think he knows we're following him?" Dru asked.

"Sure. And he knows I'm a tracker. He'll use every trick in the book now."

For a while, the trail was not difficult to follow, and they rode again. Mike Bastian could not take his mind from the girl who rode with him. What would she think when she discovered her father was an outlaw—that he was the mysterious leader of the outlaws?

X

Pine trees thinned out, and before them was the vast blue and misty distance of the cañon. Mike slid to the ground and walked slowly forward on moccasined feet. There were a few scattered pines and the cracked and splintered rim of the cañon, breaking sharply off to fall away into the vast depths. Carefully he scouted the edge of the cañon, and, when he saw the trail, he stopped, flat-footed, and stared, his heart in his mouth.

Had they gone down *there?* He knelt on the rock. Yes, there was the scar of a horse's hoof. He walked out a little farther, looking down.

The cliff fell away for hundreds of feet without even a hump in the wall. Then, just a little farther along, he saw the trail. It was a rocky ledge scarcely three feet wide that ran steeply down the side of the rock from the cañon's rim. On the left the wall, on the right the vast, astonishing emptiness of the cañon.

Thoughtfully he walked back and explained.

"All right, Mike." Dru nodded. "If you're ready, I am."

He hesitated to bring the horses, but decided it would be the best thing. He drew his rifle from the saddle scabbard and jacked a shell into the chamber.

Dru looked at him, steady-eyed. "Mike, maybe he'll be waiting for us," she said. "We may get shot. Especially you."

Bastian nodded. "That could be," he agreed.

She came toward him. "Mike, who are you? What are you? Uncle Voyle seemed to know you, or about you, and that outlaw, Perrin. He knew you. Then I heard you say Ben Curry had sent you to stop them from raiding the ranch. Are you an outlaw, Mike?"

For as long as a man might have counted a slow ten, Mike stared out over the cañon, trying to make up his mind. Now, at this stage, there was only one thing he could say.

"No, Dru, not exactly, but I was raised by an outlaw," he explained. "Ben Curry brought me up like his own son, with the idea that I would take over the gang when he stepped out."

"You lived with them in their hide-out?"

"When I wasn't out in the woods." He nodded. "Ben Curry had me taught everything . . . how to shoot, to track, to ride, even to open safes and locks."

"What's he like, this Ben Curry?" Dru asked.

"He's quite a man," Mike Bastian said, smiling. "When he started outlawing, everybody was rustling a few cows, and he just went a step further and robbed banks and stages, or planned the robberies and directed them. I don't expect he really figured himself bad. He might have done a lot of other things, for he has brains. But he killed a man . . . and then, in getting away, he killed another. The first one was justified. The second one . . . well, he was in a hurry."

"Are you apologizing for him?" Dru said quickly. "After all, he was an outlaw and a killer."

He glanced at her. "He was, yes. And I am not making any apologies for him, nor would he want them. He's a man who always stood on his own two feet. Maybe he was wrong but there were the circumstances. And he was mighty good to me. I didn't have a home, no place to go, and he took me in and treated me right."

"Was he a big man, Mike? A big old man?"

He did not look her way. She knew, then?

"In many ways," he said, "he is one of the biggest men I know. We'd better get started."

It was like stepping off into space, yet the horses took it calmly enough. They were mountain bred and would go anywhere as long as they could get a foothold on something.

The red maw of the cañon gaped to receive them, and they went down, following the narrow, switchback trail that seemed to be leading them into the very center of the earth.

It was late afternoon before they started down, and now the shadows began to creep up the cañon walls, reaching with ghostly fingers for the vanished sunlight. Overhead the red blazed with the setting sun's reflection and seemed to be hurling arrows of flame back into the sky. The depths of the cañon seemed chill after the sun on the plateau, and Mike walked warily, always a little ahead of the horse he was leading.

Dru was riding, and, when he glanced back once, she smiled brightly at him, keeping her eyes averted from the awful depths below.

Mike had no flair for making love, for his knowledge of women was slight. He wished now that he knew more of their ways, knew the things to say that would appeal to a girl.

A long time later they reached the bottom, and far away on their right they could hear the river rushing through the cañon. Mike knelt, and, striking a match, he studied the trail. The tracks turned back into a long cañon that led back from the river.

He got into the saddle then, his rifle across his saddle, and rode forward.

At the end, it was simple. The long chase had led to a quiet meadow, and he could smell the grass before he reached it, could hear the babble of a small stream. The cañon walls flared wide, and he saw, not far away, the faint sparkle of a fire.

Dru came alongside him. "Is . . . that them?" she asked, low-voiced.

"It couldn't be anyone else." Her hand was on his arm and he put his own hand over it. "I've got to go up there alone, Dru. I'll have to kill him, you know."

"Yes," she said simply, "but don't *you* be killed." He started to ride forward, and she caught his arm. "Mike, why have you done all this?" she asked. "She isn't your sister."

"No." He looked very serious in the vague light. "She's yours."

He turned his head and spoke to the horse. The animal started forward.

When, shortly, he stopped the mount, he heard a sound nearby. Dru Ragan was close behind him.

"Dru," he whispered, "you've *got* to stay back. Hold my horse. I'm going up on foot."

He left her like that and walked steadily forward. Even before he got to the fire, he could see them. The girl, her head slumped over on her arms, half dead with weariness, and Ducrow, bending over the fire. From time to time Ducrow glanced at the girl. Finally he reached over and cuffed her on the head.

"Come on, get some of this coffee into you," he growled. "This is where we stay . . . in Peach

136

Meadow Cañon. Might as well give up seein' that sister of yours, because you're my woman now." He sneered. "Monson and them, they ran like scared foxes. No bottom to them. I come for a woman, and I got one."

"Why don't you let me go?" Juliana protested. "My father will pay you well. He has lots of money."

"Your pa?" Ducrow stared at her. "I thought Voyle Ragan was your uncle?"

"He is. I mean Ben Ragan. He ranches up north of the cañon."

"North of the cañon?" Ducrow laughed. "Not unless he's a Mormon, he don't. What's he look like, this pa of yours?"

"He's a great big man, with iron-gray hair, a heavy jaw. . . ." She stopped, staring at Ducrow. "What's the matter with you?"

Ducrow got slowly to his feet. "Your pa . . . Ben Ragan? A big man with gray hair, an' maybe a scar on his jaw . . . that him?"

"Oh, yes. Take me to him. He'll pay you well."

Suddenly Ducrow let out a guffaw of laughter. He slapped his leg and bellowed. "Man, oh, man! Is that a good one! You're Ben Curry's daughter! Why, that old. . . ." He sobered. "What did you call him? Ragan? Why, honey, that old man of yours is the biggest outlaw in the world. Or was until today. Well, of all the. . . ."

"You've laughed enough, Ducrow!"

As Mike Bastian spoke, he stepped to the edge of the firelight.

"You leave a tough trail, but I followed it."

Ducrow turned, half crouching, his cruel eyes glaring at Bastian.

"Roundy was right," he snarled. "You could track a snake across a flat rock! Well, now that you're here, what are you goin' to do?"

"That depends on you, Ducrow. You can drop your guns, and I'll take you in for a trial. Or you can shoot it out."

"Drop my guns?" Ducrow chuckled. "You'd actually take me in, too! You're too soft, Bastian. You'd never make the boss man old Ben Curry was. He would never even've said yes or no. He would have seen me and gone to blastin'! You got a sight to learn, youngster. Too bad you ain't goin' to live long enough to learn it."

Ducrow lifted one hand carelessly and wiped it across the tobacco-stained stubble of his beard. His right hand swept down for his gun even as his left touched his face. His gun came up, spouting flame.

Mike Bastian palmed his gun and momentarily held it rigid. Then he fired.

Ducrow winced like he had been slugged in the chest, and then he lifted on his tiptoes. His gun came level again. "You're . . . fast," he gasped. "Devilish fast."

He fired, and then Mike triggered his gun once

more. The second shot spun Ducrow around and he fell, face down, at the edge of the fire.

Dru came running, her rifle in her hand, but when she saw Mike still standing, she dropped the rifle and ran to him. "Oh, Mike!" she sobbed. "I was so frightened! I thought you were killed!"

Julie started to rise, and then fell headlong in a faint. Dru rushed to her side.

Mike Bastian absently thumbed shells into his gun and stared down at the fallen man. He had killed a third man. Suddenly, and profoundly, he wished with all his heart he would never have to kill another.

He holstered his weapon and, gathering up the dead man, carried him away from the fire. He would bury him here, in Peach Meadow Cañon.

XI

Sunlight lay upon the empty street of the settlement in Toadstool Cañon when Mike Bastian, his rifle crosswise on his saddle, rode slowly into the lower end of the town.

Beside him, sitting straight in her saddle, rode Dru Ragan. Julie had stayed at the ranch, but Dru had flatly refused. Ben Curry was her father, and she was going to him, outlaw camp or not.

If Dave Lenaker had arrived, Mike thought, he was quiet enough, for there was no sound. No horses stood at the hitch rails, and the doors of the saloon were wide open.

Something fluttered on the ground, and Mike looked at it quickly. It was a torn bit of cloth on a man's body. The man was a stranger. Dru noticed it and her face paled.

His rifle at ready, Mike rode on, eyes shifting from side to side. A man's wrist lay in sight across a window sill, his pistol on the porch outside. There was blood on the stoop of another house.

"There's been a fight," Mike said, "and a bad one. You'd better get set for the worst."

Dru said nothing, but her mouth held firm. At the last building, the mess hall, a man lay dead in a doorway. They rode on, and then drew up at the foot of the stone steps, and dismounted. Mike shoved his rifle back in the saddle scabbard and loosened his six-guns.

"Let's go," he said.

The wide verandah was empty and still, but when he stepped into the huge living room, he stopped in amazement. Five men sat about a table playing cards.

Ben Curry's head came up and he waved at them. "Come on in, Mike!" he called. "Who's that with you? Dru, by all that's holy!"

Doc Sawyer, Roundy, Garlin, and Colley were there. Garlin's head was bandaged, and Colley had one foot stretched out, stiff and straight, as did Ben Curry. But all were smiling.

Dru ran to her father and fell on her knees beside him.

"Oh, Dad!" she cried. "We were so scared!"

"What happened here?" Mike demanded. "Don't sit there grinning! Did Dave Lenaker come?"

"He sure did, and what do you think?" Doc said. "It was Rigger Molina got him! Rigger got to Weaver and found out Perrin had double-crossed him before he ever pulled the job. He discovered that Perrin had lied about the guards, so he rushed back. When he found out that Ben was crippled and that Kerb Perrin had run out, he waited for Lenaker himself.

"He was wonderful, Mike," Doc continued. "I never saw anything like it! He paced the verandah out there like a bear in a cage, swearing and waiting for Lenaker. Muttered . . . 'Leave you in the lurch, will they? I'll show 'em! Lenaker thinks he can gun you down because you're gettin' old, does he? Well, killer I may be, but I can kill him!' And he did, Mike. They shot it out in the street down there. Dave Lenaker, as slim and tall as you, and that great bear of a Molina.

"Lenaker beat him to the draw," Doc went on. "He got two bullets into the Rigger, but Molina wouldn't go down. He stood there, spraddle-legged, in the street and shot until both guns were empty. Lenaker kept shooting and must have hit Molina five times, but when he went down, Rigger walked over to him and spat in his face. 'That's for double-crossers!' he said. He was magnificent!"

"They fooled me, Mike," Roundy said. "I seen trouble a-comin' an' figured I'd better get to old Ben. I never figured they'd slip in behind you like they done. Then the news of Lenaker comin' got me. I knowed him an' was afraid of him, so I figured in order to save Ben Curry I'd get down the road and dry-gulch him. Never killed a gunslinger like him in my life, Mike, but I was sure aimin' to. But he got by me on another trail. After Molina killed Lenaker, his boys and some of them from here started after the gold they'd figured was in this house."

"Doc here," Garlin said, "is some fighter. I didn't know he had it in him."

"Roundy, Doc, Garlin, an' me," Colley said, "we sided Ben Curry. It was a swell scrap while it lasted. Garlin got one through his scalp, and I got two bullets in the leg. Aside from that, we came out all right."

Briefly, then, Mike explained all that had transpired, how he had killed Perrin, and then had trailed Ducrow to Peach Meadow Cañon and the fight there.

"Where's the gang?" he demanded now. "All gone?"

"All the live ones." Ben Curry nodded grimly. "There's a few won't go anywhere. Funny, the only man who ever fooled me was Rigger Molina. I never knew the man was that loyal, yet he stood by me when I was in no shape to fight Lenaker. Took that fight right off my hands. He soaked up lead like a sponge soaks water."

Ben Curry looked quickly at Dru. "So you know you're the daughter of an outlaw? Well, I'm sorry, Dru. I never aimed for you to know. I was gettin' shet of this business and planned to settle down on a ranch with your mother and live out the rest of my days plumb peaceful."

"Why don't you?" Dru demanded.

He looked at her, his admiring eyes taking in her slim, well-rounded figure. "You reckon she'll have me?" he asked. "She looked a sight like you when she was younger, Dru."

"Of course, she'll have you. She doesn't know . . . or didn't know until Julie told her. But I think she guessed. *I* knew. I saw you talking with some men once, and later heard they were outlaws, and then I began hearing about Ben Curry."

Curry looked thoughtfully from Dru to Mike.

"Is there something between you two? Or am I an old fool?"

Mike flushed and kept his eyes away from Dru.

"He's a fine man, Dru," Doc Sawyer said. "And well educated, if I do say so . . . who taught him all he knows."

"All he knows!" Roundy stared at Doc with contempt. "Book larnin'! Where would that gal be but for what I told him? How to read sign, how to foller a trail? Where would she be?"

Mike took Dru out to the verandah then.

"I can read sign, all right," he said, "but I'm no hand at reading the trail to a woman's heart. You would have to help me, Dru."

She laughed softly, and her eyes were bright as she slipped her arm through his. "Why, Mike, you've been blazing a trail over and back and up again, ever since I met you in the street at Weaver." Suddenly she sobered. "Mike, let's get some cattle and go back to Peach Meadow Cañon. You said you could make a better trail in, and it would be a wonderful place. Just you and I and. . . ."

"Sure," he said. "In Peach Meadow Cañon."

Roundy craned his head toward the door, and then he chuckled.

"That youngster," he said. "He may not know all the trails, but he sure gets where he's goin'. He sure does!"

Riding for the Brand

He had been watching the covered wagon for more than an hour. There had been no movement, no sound. The bodies of the two animals that had drawn the wagon lay in the grass, plainly visible. Farther away, almost a mile away, stood a lone buffalo bull, black against the gray distance.

Nothing moved near the wagon, but Jed Asbury had lived too long in Indian country to risk his scalp on appearances, and he knew an Indian could lie ghost-still for hours on end. He had no intention of taking such a chance, stark naked and without weapons.

Two days before he had been stripped to the hide by Indians and forced to run the gauntlet, but he had run better than they had expected and had escaped with only a few minor wounds.

Now, miles away, he had reached the limit of his endurance. Despite little water and less food he was still in traveling condition except for his feet. They were lacerated and swollen, caked with dried blood.

Warily he started forward, taking advantage of every bit of cover and moving steadily toward the wagon. When he was within fifty feet, he settled down in the grass to study the situation.

This was the scene of an attack. Evidently the wagon had been alone, and the bodies of two men

145

and a woman lay stretched on the grass. Clothing, papers, and cooking utensils were scattered, evidence of a hasty looting. Whatever had been the dreams of these people, they were ended now, another sacrifice to the westward march of empire. And the dead would not begrudge him what he needed.

Rising from the grass, he went cautiously to the wagon, a tall, powerfully muscled young man, unshaven and untrimmed.

He avoided the bodies. Oddly they were not mutilated, which was unusual, and the men still wore their boots. As a last resort he would take a pair for himself. First, he must examine the wagon.

If Indians had looted the wagon, they had done so hurriedly, for the interior of the wagon was in the wildest state of confusion. In the bottom of a trunk he found a fine black broadcloth suit as well as a new pair of hand-tooled leather boots, a woolen shirt, and several white shirts.

"Somebody's Sunday-go-to-meetin' outfit," he muttered. "Hadn't better try the boots on the way my feet are swollen."

He found clean underwear and dressed, putting on some rougher clothes that he found in the same chest. When he was dressed enough to protect him from the sun, he took water from a half empty barrel on the side of the wagon and bathed his feet; then he bandaged them with strips of white cloth torn from a dress.

His feet felt much better, and, as the boots were a size larger than he usually wore, he tried them. There was some discomfort, but he could wear them.

With a shovel tied to the wagon's side, he dug a grave and buried the three side-by-side, covered them with quilts from the wagon, filled in the earth, and piled stones over the grave. Then, hat in hand, he recited the Twenty-Third Psalm.

The savages or whoever had killed them had made only a hasty search, so now he went to the wagon to find whatever might be useful to him or might inform him as to the identity of the dead.

There were some legal papers, a will, and a handful of letters. Putting these to one side with a poncho he found, he spotted a sewing basket. Remembering his grandmother's habits, he emptied out the needles and thread, and under the padded bottom of the basket he found a large sealed envelope.

Ripping it open, he grunted with satisfaction. Wrapped in carefully folded tissue paper were twenty $20 gold pieces. Pocketing them, he delved deeper into the trunk. He found more carefully folded clothes. Several times he broke off his searching of the wagon to survey the country about, but saw nothing. The wagon was in a concealed situation where a rider might have passed within a few yards and not seen it. He seemed to have approached from the only angle from which it was visible.

In the very bottom of the trunk he struck pay dirt. He found a steel box. With a pick he forced it open. Inside, on folded velvet, lay a magnificent set of pistols, silver-plated and beautifully engraved, with pearl handles. Wrapped in a towel nearby he found a pair of black leather cartridge belts and twin holsters. With them was a sack of .44 cartridges. Promptly he loaded the guns, and then stuffed the loops of both cartridge belts. After that, he tried the balance of the guns. The rest of the cartridges he dropped into his pockets.

In another fold of the cloth he found a pearl-handled knife of finely tempered steel, a Spanish fighting knife and a beautiful piece of work. He slung the scabbard around his neck with the haft just below his collar.

Getting his new possessions together, he made a pack of the clothing inside the poncho and used string to make a back pack of it. In the inside pocket of the coat he stowed the legal papers and the letters. In his hip pocket he stuffed a small leather-bound book he had found among the scattered contents of the wagon. He read little, but knew the value of a good book.

He had had three years of intermittent schooling, learning to read, write, and cipher a little.

There was a canteen and he filled it. Rummaging in the wagon he found the grub box almost empty, a little coffee, some moldy bread, and nothing else useful. He took the coffee, a small pot, and a tin cup. Then he glanced at the sun and started away.

Jed Asbury was accustomed to fending for himself. That there could be anything wrong in appropriating what he had found never entered his head, nor would it have entered the head of any other man at the time. Life was hard, and one lived as best one might. If the dead had any heirs, there would be a clue in the letters or the will. He would pay them when he could. No man would begrudge him taking what was needed to survive, but to repay the debt incurred was a foregone conclusion.

Jed had been born on an Ohio farm, his parents dying when he was ten years old. He had been sent to a crabbed uncle living in a Maine fishing village. For three years his uncle worked him like a slave, sending him out on the Banks with a fishing boat. Finally Jed had abandoned the boat, deep-sea fishing, and his uncle.

He had walked to Boston and by devious methods reached Philadelphia. He had run errands, worked in a mill, and then gotten a job as a printer's devil. He had grown to like a man who came often to the shop, a quiet man with dark hair and large gray eyes, his head curiously wide across the temples. The man wrote stories and literary criticism and occasionally loaned Jed books to read. His name was Edgar Poe and he was reported to be the foster son of John Allan, said to be the richest man in Virginia.

When Jed left the print shop, it was to ship on a windjammer for a voyage around the Horn. From San Francisco he had gone to Australia for a year in the gold fields, and then to South Africa and back to New York. He was twenty then and a big, well-made young man hardened by the life he had lived. He had gone on a riverboat down the Mississippi to Natchez and New Orleans.

In New Orleans, Jem Mace had taught him to box. Until then all he had known about fighting had been acquired through rough-and-tumble. From New Orleans he had gone to Havana, to Brazil, and then back to the States. In Natchez he had caught a cardsharp cheating. Jed Asbury had proved a bit quicker, and the gambler died, a victim of six-shooter justice. Jed left town just ahead of several of the gambler's irate companions.

On a Missouri River steamboat he had gone up to Fort Benton and then overland to Bannock. He had traveled with wagon freighters to Laramie, and then to Dodge.

In Tascosa he had encountered a brother of the dead Natchez gambler accompanied by two of the irate companions. He had killed two of his enemies and wounded the other, coming out of the fracas with a bullet in his leg. He traveled on to Santa Fe.

At twenty-four he was footloose and looking for a destination. Working as a bullwhacker he made a round trip to Council Bluffs, and then joined a wagon train for Cheyenne. The Comanches, raiding north, had interfered, and he had been the sole survivor.

He knew about where he was now, somewhere south and west of Dodge, but probably closer to Santa Fe than to the trail town. He should not be far from the cattle trail leading past Tascosa, so he headed that way. Along the river bottoms there should be strays lost from previous herds, so he could eat until a trail herd came along.

Walking a dusty trail in the heat, he shifted his small pack constantly and kept turning to scan the country over which he had come. He was in the heart of Indian country.

On the morning of the third day he sighted a trail herd, headed for Kansas. As he walked toward the herd, two of the three horsemen riding point turned toward him.

One was a lean, red-faced man with a yellowed mustache and a gleam of quizzical humor around his eyes. The other was a stocky, friendly rider on a paint horse.

"Howdy!" The older man's voice was amused. "Out for a mornin' stroll?"

"By courtesy of a bunch of Comanches. I was bullwhacking with a wagon train out of Santa Fe for Cheyenne and we had a little Winchester

151

arbitration. They held the high cards." Briefly he explained.

"You'll want a hoss. Ever work cattle?"

"Here and there. D'you need a hand?"

"Forty a month and all you can eat."

"The coffee's a fright," the other rider said. "That dough wrangler never learned to make coffee that didn't taste like strong lye."

That night in camp Jed Asbury got out the papers he had found in the wagon. He read the first letter he opened.

Dear Michael,

When you get this you will know George is dead. He was thrown from a horse near Willow Springs, dying the following day. The home ranch comprises 60,000 acres and the other ranches twice that. This is to be yours or your heirs if you have married since we last heard from you, if you or the heirs reach the place within one year of George's death. If you do not claim your estate within that time, the property will be inherited by next of kin. You may remember what Walt is like, from the letters.

Naturally we hope you will come at once for we all know what it would be like if Walt took over. You should be around twenty-six now and able to handle Walt, but be careful. He is dangerous and has killed several men.

Things are in good shape now but trouble is impending with Besovi, a neighbor of ours. If Walt takes over, that will certainly happen. Also, those of us who have worked and lived here so long will be thrown out.

Tony Costa

The letter had been addressed to Michael Latch, St. Louis, Missouri. Thoughtfully Jed folded the letter and then glanced through the others. He learned much, yet not enough.

Michael Latch had been the nephew of George Baca, a half-American, half-Spanish rancher who owned a huge *hacienda* in California. Neither Baca nor Tony Costa had ever seen Michael. Nor had the man named Walt, who apparently was the son of George's half-brother. The will was that of Michael's father, Thomas Latch, and conveyed to Michael the deed to a small California ranch.

From other papers and an unmailed letter, Jed discovered that the younger of the two men he had buried had been Michael Latch. The other dead man and the woman had been Randy and May Kenner. There was mention in a letter of a girl named Arden who had accompanied them.

The Indians must have taken her with them, Jed mused. He considered trying to find her, but dismissed the idea as impractical. Looking for a needle in a haystack would at least be a local job, but trying to find one of many roving bands of Comanches would be well nigh impossible. Nevertheless, he would inform the Army and the trading posts. Often, negotiations could be started, and for an appropriate trade in goods she might be recovered, if still living.

Then he had another idea. Michael Latch was dead. A vast estate awaited him, a fine, comfortable, constructive life, which young Latch would have loved. Now the estate would fall to Walt, whoever he was, unless he, Jed Asbury, took the name of Michael Latch and claimed the estate.

The man who was his new boss rode in from a ride around the herd. He glanced at Jed, who was putting the letters away. "What did you say your name was?"

Only for an instant did Jed hesitate. "Latch," he replied, "Michael Latch."

Warm sunlight lay upon the *hacienda* called Casa Grande. The hounds sprawling in drowsy peace under the smoke trees scarcely opened their eyes when the tall stranger turned his horse through the gate. Many strangers came to Casa Grande, and the uncertainty that hung over the vast ranch had not reached the dogs.

Tony Costa straightened his lean frame from the doorway and studied the stranger from under an eye-shielding hand.

"*Señorita*, someone comes!"

"Is it Walt?" Sharp, quick heels sounded on the flagstoned floor. "What will we do? Oh, if Michael were only here!"

"Today is the last day," Costa said gloomily.

"Look!" The girl touched his arm. "Right behind him! That's Walt Seever!"

"Two men with him. We will have trouble if we try to stop him, *señorita*. He would not lose the ranch to a woman."

The stranger on the black horse swung down at the steps. He wore a flat-crowned black hat and a black broadcloth suit. His boots were almost new and hand-tooled, but when her eyes dropped to the guns, she gasped. "Tony! The guns!"

The young man came up the steps, swept off his hat, and bowed. "You are Tony Costa? The foreman of Casa Grande?"

The other riders clattered into the court, and their leader, a big man with bold, hard eyes, swung down. He brushed past the stranger and confronted the foreman.

"Well, Costa, today this ranch becomes mine, and you're fired!"

"I think not."

All eyes turned to the stranger. The girl's eyes were startled, suddenly cautious. This man was strong, she thought suddenly, and he was not afraid. He had a clean-cut face, pleasant gray eyes, and a certain assurance born of experience.

"If you are Walt," the stranger said, "you can ride back where you came from. This ranch is mine. I am Michael Latch."

Fury struggled with shocked disbelief in the expression on Walt Seever's face. "You? Michael Latch? You couldn't be!"

"Why not?" Jed was calm. Eyes on Seever, he could not see the effect of his words on Costa or the girl. "George sent for me. Here I am."

Mingled with the baffled rage, there was something else in Walt's face, some ugly suspicion or knowledge. Suddenly Jed suspected that Walt knew he was not Michael Latch. Or doubted it vehemently.

Tony Costa had moved up beside him. "Why not? We have expected him. His uncle wrote for him, and after Baca's death I wrote to him. If you doubt it, look at the guns. Are there two such pairs of guns in the world? Are there two men in the world who could make such guns?"

Seever's eyes went to the guns, and Jed saw doubt and puzzlement replace the angry certainty.

"I'll have to have more proof than a pair of guns."

Jed took the letter from his pocket and passed it over. "From Tony. I also have my father's will and other letters."

Walt Seever glanced at the letter and then hurled it into the dust. "Let's get out of here!" He started for his horse.

Jed Asbury watched them go, puzzling over that odd reaction of Walt's. Until Seever saw that letter, he had been positive Jed was not Michael Latch. Now he was no longer sure. But what could have made him so positive in the beginning? What could he know?

The girl was whispering something to Costa. Jed turned, smiling at her. "I don't believe Walt was too happy at my being here," he said.

"No"—Costa's expression was unrevealing— "he isn't. He expected to have this ranch for himself." Costa turned toward the girl. "*Señor* Latch? I would introduce to you *Señorita* Carol James, a . . . a ward of *Señor* Baca's and his good friend."

Jed acknowledged the introduction.

"You must bring me up to date. I want to know all you can tell me about Walt Seever."

Costa exchanged a glance with Carol. "Of course, *señor*. Walt Seever is a *malo hombre*, *señor*. He has killed several men, is most violent. The men with him were Harry Strykes and Gin Feeley. They are gunmen and believed to be thieves."

Jed Asbury listened attentively, yet wondered about Carol's reaction. Did she suspect he was not Michael Latch? Did she know he was not Latch? If so, why didn't she say something?

He was surprised they had accepted him so readily, for even after he had decided to take the

157

dead man's place he had not been sure he could go through with it. He had a feeling of guilt and some shame, yet the real Michael Latch was dead, and the only man he was depriving seemed to be a thoroughly bad one whose first action would have been to fire the ranch's foreman, a man whose home had always been this *hacienda*.

He had made a wild ride over rough country to get here in time, but over all that distance he had debated with himself about the rights and the wrongs of his action. He was nobody, a drifter, worker at whatever came to hand, an adventurer, if you will, but not unlike hundreds of others who came and went across the West and more often than not left their bones in the wilderness, their flesh to feed the ancient soil.

He had not known Michael Latch, or what kind of man he had been, but he suspected he had been a good man and a trusted one. Why could he not save the ranch from Walt Seever, find a home for himself at last, and be the kind of man Michael Latch would have been?

All through that wild ride West he had struggled with his conscience, trying to convince himself that what he did was the right thing. He could do Latch no harm, and Costa and Carol seemed pleased to have him here, now that he had arrived. The expression on Seever's face had been worth the ride, if nothing more.

There was something else that disturbed him.

That was Walt Seever's odd reaction when he had said he was Michael Latch.

"You say," Jed turned to Carol, "that Seever was sure he would inherit?"

She nodded. "Yes, though until about three months ago he was hating George Baca for leaving the ranch to you. Then suddenly he changed his mind and seemed sure he would inherit, that you would never come to claim your inheritance."

It had been about three months ago that Jed Asbury had come upon the lone wagon and the murdered people, a murder he had laid to Indians. But leaving the corpses with their clothing and the wagon unlooted did not seem like any raiding parties of which he had known. Three people murdered—could Seever have known of that? Was that why he had suddenly been sure he would inherit?

The idea took root. Seever must have known of the killings. If that was so, then the three had not been killed by Indians, and a lot remained to be explained. How did the wagon happen to be alone, so far from anywhere? And what had become of the girl, Arden?

If Indians had not made the attack and carried Arden off, then somebody else had captured her, and wherever she was she would know he was not the real Michael Latch. She would know Jed Asbury for an imposter, but she might also know who the killers were.

Walking out on the wide terrace overlooking the green valley beyond the ranch house, Jed stared down the valley, his mind filled with doubts and apprehensions.

It was a lovely land, well watered and rich. Here, with what he knew of land and cattle, he could carry on the work George Baca had begun. He would do what Michael Latch would have done, and he might even do it better.

There was danger, but when had he not known danger? And these people at the ranch were good people, honest people. If he did not do more than save the ranch from Seever and his lawless crowd, he would have adequate reason for taking the place of the dead man. Yet he was merely finding excuses for his conduct.

The guns he wore meant something, too. Carol had recognized them, and so had Seever. What was their significance?

He was in deep water here. Every remark he made must be guarded. Even if they had not seen him before, there must be family stories and family tradition of which he knew nothing. There was a movement behind him, and Jed Asbury turned. In the gathering dusk he saw Carol.

"Do you like it?" She gestured toward the valley.

"It's splendid. I have never seen anything prettier. A man could do a lot with land like that. It could be a paradise."

"Somehow you are different than I expected."

160

"I am?" He was careful, waiting for her to say more.

"You're much more assured than I expected you to be. Mike was quiet, Uncle George used to say. Read a lot, but did not get around much. You startled me by the way you handled Walt Seever."

He shrugged. "A man changes. He grows older, and coming West to a new life makes a man more sure of himself."

She noticed the book in his pocket. "What book do you have?" she asked curiously.

It was a battered copy of Plutarch. He was on safe ground here, for on the flyleaf was written: *To Michael, from Uncle George.*

He showed it to her and she said: "It was a favorite of Uncle George's. He used to say that next to the Bible more great men had read Plutarch than any other book."

"I like it. I've been reading it nights." He turned to face her. "Carol, what do you think Walt Seever will do?"

"Try to kill you or have you killed," she replied. She gestured toward the guns. "You had better learn to use those."

"I can, a little."

He dared not admit how well he could use them, for a man does not come by such skill overnight, nor the cool nerve it takes to use them facing an armed enemy. "Seever has counted on this place, has he?"

161

"He has made a lot of talk." She glanced up at him. "You know, Walt was no blood relation to Uncle George. He was the son of a woman of the gold camps who married George Baca's half-brother."

"I see." Actually Walt Seever's claim was scarcely better than his own. "I know from the letters that Uncle George wanted me to have the estate, but I feel like an outsider. I am afraid I may be doing wrong to take a ranch built by the work of other people. Walt may have more right to it than I. I may be doing wrong to assert my claim."

He was aware of her searching gaze. When she spoke, it was deliberately and as if she had reached some decision.

"Michael, I don't know you, but you would have to be very bad, indeed, to be as dangerous and evil as Walt Seever. I would say that no matter what the circumstances, you should stay and see this through."

Was there a hint that she might know more than she admitted? Yet it was natural that he should be looking for suspicion behind every phrase. Yet he must do that or be trapped.

"However, it is only fair to warn you that you have let yourself in for more than you could expect. Uncle George knew very well what you would be facing. He knew the viciousness of Walt Seever. He doubted you would be clever or bold enough to defeat Seever. So I must warn you,

Michael Latch, that, if you do stay, and I believe you should, you will probably be killed."

He smiled into the darkness. Since boyhood he had lived in proximity to death. He was not foolhardy or reckless, for a truly brave man was never reckless. He knew he could skirt the ragged edge of death if need be. He had been there before.

He was an interloper here, yet the man whose place he had taken was dead, and perhaps he could carry on in his place, making the ranch safe for those who loved it. Then he could move on and leave this ranch to Carol and to the care of Tony Costa.

He turned. "I am tired," he said. "I have ridden long and hard to get here. Now I'd like to rest." He paused. "But I shall stay, at least. . . ."

Jed Asbury was already fast asleep when Carol went into the dining room where Tony Costa sat at the long table. Without him, what would she have done? What could she have done? He had worked with her father for thirty years and had lived on the *hacienda* all his life, and he was past sixty now. He still stood as erect and slender as he had when a young man. And he was shrewd.

Costa looked up. He was drinking coffee by the light of a candle. "For better or worse, *señorita*, it has begun. What do you think now?"

"He told me, after I warned him, that he would stay."

Costa studied the coffee in his cup. "You are not afraid?"

"No. He faced Walt Seever and that was enough for me. Anything is to be preferred to Walt Seever."

"*Sí.*" Costa's agreement was definite. "*Señorita*, did you notice his hands when he faced Seever. They were ready, Carolita, ready to draw. This man has used a gun before. He is a strong man, Carolita."

"Yes, I think you are right. He is a strong man."

For two days nothing happened from the direction of town. Walt Seever and his hard-bitten companions might have vanished from the earth, but on the Rancho Casa Grande much was happening, and Tony Costa was whistling most of the time.

Jed Asbury's formal education was slight, but he knew men, how to lead them, and how best to get results. Above all, he had practical knowledge of handling cattle and of range conditions.

He was up at 5:00 the morning after his discussion with Carol, and, when she awakened, old María, the cook, told her the *Señor* was hard at work in his office. The door was open a crack, and, as she passed by, she glimpsed him deep in the accounts of the ranch. Pinned up before him was a map of the Casa Grande holdings, and, as he checked the disposition of the cattle, he studied the map.

He ate a hurried breakfast and at 8:00 was in the

saddle. He ate his next meal at a line camp and rode in long after dark. In two days he spent twenty hours in the saddle.

On the third day he called Costa to the office and sent María to request the presence of Carol. Puzzled and curious, she joined them.

Jed wore a white shirt, black trousers, and the silver guns. His face seemed to have thinned down in just the two days, but, when he glanced at her, he smiled.

"You have been here longer than I and are, in a sense, a partner." Before she could interrupt, he turned to Costa. "I want you to remain as foreman. However, I have asked you both to be here as I plan some changes." He indicated a point on the map. "That narrow passage leads into open country and then desert. I found cattle tracks there, going out. It might be rustlers. A little blasting up in the rocks will close that gap."

"It is a good move," Costa agreed.

"This field . . ."—Jed indicated a large area in a field not far from the house—"must be fenced off. We will plant it to flax."

"Flax, *señor?*"

"There will be a good market for it." He indicated a smaller area. "This piece we will plant to grapes, and all that hillside will support them. There will be times when we cannot depend on cattle or horses, so there must be other sources of income."

Carol watched in wonderment. He was moving fast, this new Michael Latch. He had grasped the situation at once and was moving to make changes that Uncle George had only thought about.

"Also, Costa, we must have a roundup. Gather the cattle and cut out all those over four years old, and we'll sell them. I saw a lot of cattle from five to eight years old back there in the brush."

After he had ridden away to study another quarter of the ranch, Carol walked to the blacksmith shop to talk to Pat Flood. He was an old seafaring man with a peg leg who Uncle George had found broke and on the beach in San Francisco and who had proved to be a marvel with tools.

He looked up from under his bushy brows as she stopped at the shop. He was cobbling a pair of boots. Before she could speak, he said: "This here new boss, Latch? Been to sea, ain't he?"

Surprised, she said: "What gave you that idea?"

"Seen him throw a bowline on a bight yesterday. Purtiest job I seen since comin' ashore. He made that rope fast like he'd been doin' it for years."

"I expect many men handle ropes well," she commented.

"Not sailor fashion. He called it a line, too. 'Hand me that line!' he says. Me, I been ashore so long I'm callin' them ropes m'self, but not him. I'd stake my supper that he's walked a deck."

· · ·

Jed Asbury was riding to town. He wanted to assay the feeling of the townspeople toward the ranch, toward George Baca and Walt Seever. There was a chance he might talk to a few people before they discovered his connection. Also, he was irritated at the delay in the showdown with Seever. His appearance in town might force that showdown or allow Seever an opportunity if he felt he needed one. If there was to be a meeting, he wanted it over with so he could get on with work at the ranch.

He had never avoided trouble. It was his nature to go right to the heart of it, and for this trip he was wearing worn gray trousers, boots, his silver guns, and a battered black hat. He hoped they would accept him as a drifting cowpuncher.

Already, in riding around the ranch and in casual talk with the hands, he had learned a good deal. He knew the place to go in town was the Golden Strike. He tied his horse to the hitching rail and went inside.

Three men loafed at the bar. The big man with the scar on his lip was Harry Strykes, who had ridden with Seever. As Jed stepped to the bar and ordered his drink, a man seated at a table got up and went to Strykes. "Never saw him before," he said.

Strykes went around the man and faced Jed. "So? Cuttin' in for yourself, are you? Well, nobody gets in the way of my boss. Go for your gun or go back to Texas. You got a choice."

"I'm not going to kill you," Jed said. "I don't like your manner, but if you touch that gun, I'll have to blow your guts out. Instead, I'd rather teach you a lesson."

His left hand grabbed Strykes by the belt. He shoved back and then lifted, and his left toe kicked Strykes's foot from under him as Jed lifted on the belt and then let go.

The move caught Strykes unaware, and he hit the floor hard. For an instant he was shaken, but then he came off the floor with a curse.

Jed Asbury had taken up his drink with his left hand, leaning carelessly against the bar. Jed's left foot was on the brass rail, and, as Strykes swung his right fist, Jed straightened his leg, moving himself out from the bar so that the punch missed, throwing Strykes against the bar. As his chest hit the bar, Jed flipped the remainder of his drink into Strykes's eyes.

Moving away from the bar, he made no attempt to hit Strykes, just letting the man paw at the stinging whiskey in his eyes. When he seemed about to get his vision cleared, Jed leaned forward and jerked open Strykes's belt. Strykes's pants slid toward his knees, and he grabbed at them. Jed pushed him with the tips of his fingers. With his pants around his knees Strykes could not stagger, so he fell.

Jed turned to the others in the room. "Sorry to have disturbed you, gentlemen. The name is Mike Latch. If you are ever out to the Casa Grande, please feel free to call."

He walked out of the saloon, leaving laughter behind him as Strykes struggled to get up and pull his pants into place.

Yet he was remembering the man who had stepped up to Strykes, saying he had never seen Jed before. Had that man known the real Mike Latch? If Walt Seever knew of the covered wagon with its three murdered people, he would know Jed Asbury was an impostor and would be searching for a way to prove it. The vast and beautiful acres of Rancho Casa Grande were reason enough.

Riding homeward, he mulled over the problem. There was, of course, a chance of exposure, yet no one might ever come near who could actually identify him.

His brief altercation with Strykes had gotten him nowhere. He had undoubtedly been observed when riding into town, and the stranger must have known the real Latch. Nevertheless, the fight, if such it could be called, might have won a few friends. In the first place he could not imagine a man of Seever's stamp was well liked; in the second he had shown he was not anxious to get into a gun battle. Friends could be valuable in the months to come, and he was not catering to the rowdy element that would be Seever's friends.

Seever, however, would now be spoiling for a fight, and Jed might be killed. He must find a way to give Carol a strong claim on the ranch. Failing in that, he must kill Walt Seever.

Jed Asbury had never killed a man except to protect his own life or those close to him. Deliberately to hunt down and shoot a man was something he had never dreamed of doing, yet it might prove the only way he could protect Carol and Tony Costa. With a shock he realized he was thinking more of Carol than of himself, and he hardly knew her.

Apparently the stranger had known he was not Mike Latch. The next time it might be a direct accusation before witnesses. Jed considered the problem all the way home.

Unknown to Jed, Jim Pardo, one of the toughest hands on the ranch, had followed him into town. On his return, Pardo drew up before the black-smith shop and looked down at Pat Flood. The gigantic old blacksmith would have weighed well over three hundred pounds with two good legs, and he stood five inches over six feet. He rarely left the shop, as his wooden leg was always giving him trouble.

"He'll do," Pardo said, swinging down.

Flood lit his corncob pipe and waited.

"Had a run-in with Harry Strykes."

Flood drew on the pipe, knowing the story would come.

"Made a fool of Harry."

"Whup him?"

"Not like he should've, but maybe this was worse. He got him laughed at."

"Strykes will kill him for that."

Pardo rolled a cigarette and explained: "If Strykes is smart, he will leave him alone. This here Latch is no greenhorn. He's a man knows what he can do. No other would have handled it like he did. Never turned a hair when Strykes braced him. He's got sand in his gizzard, an' I'm placin' my bets that he'll prove a first-class hand with a shootin' iron. This one's had trouble before."

"He's deep," Flood said, chewing on his pipe stem. "Old George always said Latch was a book reader, an' quiet-like. Well"—Flood was thoughtful —"he's quiet enough, an' he reads books."

Tony Costa learned of the incident from Pardo, and María related the story to Carol. Jed made no reference to it at supper.

Costa hesitated after arising from the table. "*Señor*, since *Señor* Baca's death the *señorita* has permitted me to eat in the ranch house. There was often business to discuss. If you wish, I can. . . ."

"Forget it and, unless you're in a hurry, sit down. Your years on the ranch have earned you your place at the table."

Jed took up the pot and filled their cups. "Yesterday I was over in Fall Valley and I saw a lot of cattle with a Bar O brand."

"Bar O? *Ah*, they try it again. This brand, *señor*, belongs to a very big outfit. Frank Besovi's ranch. He is a big man, *señor*, a very troublesome man. Always he tries to move in on that valley, but if he takes that, he will want more. He has taken many ranches, so."

"Take some of the boys up there and throw those cattle off our range."

"There will be trouble, *señor*."

"Are you afraid of trouble, Costa?"

The foreman's face tightened. "No, *señor!*"

"Neither am I. Throw them off."

When the cowpunchers moved out in the morning, Jed mounted a horse and rode along. And there would be trouble. Jed saw that when they entered the valley.

Several riders were grouped near a big man with a black beard. Their horses all carried the Bar O brand.

"I'll talk to him, Costa. I want to hear what Besovi has to say."

"Very bad man," Costa warned.

Jed Asbury knew trouble when he saw it. Besovi and his men had come prepared for a showdown. Jed did not speak; he simply pushed his black against Besovi's gray. Anger flared in the big man's eyes. "What the hell are you tryin' to do?" he roared.

"Tell your boys to round up your Bar O cattle

and run them back over your line. If you don't, I'll make you run 'em back, afoot."

"What?" Besovi was incredulous. "You say that to me?"

"You heard me. Give the order."

"I'll see you in hell first!" Besovi shouted.

Jed Asbury knew this could be settled in two ways. If he went for a gun, there would be shooting and men would be killed. He chose the other way.

Acting so suddenly the move was unexpected, he grabbed Besovi by the beard and jerked the rancher sharply toward him, at the same time he kicked the rancher's foot loose from his stirrup, and then shoved hard. Besovi, caught unawares by the sheer unexpectedness of the attack, fell off his horse, and Jed hit the ground beside him.

Besovi came to his feet, clawing for his gun. "Afraid to fight with your hands?" Jed taunted.

Besovi glared and then unbuckled his gun belts and handed them to the nearest horseman. Jed stripped off his own gun belts and handed them to Costa.

Besovi started toward him with a crab-like movement that made Jed's eyes sharpen. He circled warily, looking the big man over.

Jed was at least thirty pounds lighter than Besovi, and it was obvious the big man had power in those mighty shoulders. But it would take more than power to win this kind of a fight. Jed moved in, feinting to get Besovi to reveal his fighting style. Besovi grabbed at his left wrist, and Jed brushed the hand aside and stiffened a left into his face.

Blood showed, and the Casa Grande men yelled. Pardo, rolling his quid of tobacco in his jaws, watched. He had seen Besovi fight before. The big man kept moving in, and Jed circled, wary. Besovi had some plan of action. He was no wild-swinging, hit-or-miss fighter.

Jed feinted again and then stabbed two lefts to Besovi's face, so fast one punch had barely landed before the other smacked home. Pardo was surprised to see how Besovi's head jerked under the impact.

Besovi moved in, and, when Jed led with another blow, the bigger man went under the punch and, leaping close, encircled Jed with his mighty arms. Jed's leap back had been too slow, and he sensed the power in that grasping clutch. If those huge arms closed around him, he would be in serious trouble, so he kicked up his feet and fell.

The unexpected fall caught Besovi off balance and he lunged over him, losing his grip. Quickly he spun, but Jed was already on his feet. Besovi swung and the blow caught Jed on the cheek bone. Jed took the punch standing, and Pardo's mouth dropped open in surprise. Nobody had ever stood up under a Besovi punch before.

Jed struck then, a left and right that landed solidly. The left opened the gash over Besovi's eye a little wider, and the right caught him on the chin, staggering him. Jed moved in, landing both fists to the face. The big man's hands came up to protect his face and Jed slugged him in the stomach.

Besovi got an arm around Jed and hooked him twice in the face with wicked, short punches. Jed butted him in the face with his head, breaking free.

Yet he did not step back but caught the rancher behind the head with his left hand and jerked his head down to meet a smashing right uppercut that broke Besovi's nose.

Jed pushed him away quickly and hit him seven fast punches before Besovi could get set. Like a huge, blind bear Besovi tried to swing, but Jed ducked the punch and slammed both fists to the body.

Besovi staggered, almost falling, and Jed stepped back. "You've had plenty, Besovi, and you're too good a fighter to kill. I could kill you with my fists, but I'd probably ruin my hands in doing it. Will you take those cattle and get out of here?"

Besovi, unsteady on his feet, wiped the blood from his eyes. "Well, I'll be damned! I never thought the man lived. . . . Will you shake hands?"

"I'd never shake with a tougher man or a better one."

Their hands gripped, and suddenly Besovi began to laugh. "Come over to supper some night, will you? Ma's been tellin' me this would happen. She'll be pleased to meet you." He turned to his riders. "The fun's over, boys! Round up our stock an' let's go home."

The big rancher's lips were split; there was a cut over his right eye and another under it. The other eye was swelling shut. There was one bruise on Jed's cheek bone that would be bigger tomorrow, but it wasn't enough to show he had been in a fight.

"Can't figure him," Pardo told Flood later. "Is he scared to use his guns? Or does he just like to fight with his hands?"

"He's smart," Flood suggested. "Look, he's made a friend of Besovi. If he'd beaten him to the ground, Besovi might never have forgiven him. He was savin' face for Besovi just like they do it over China way. And what if he'd gone for his guns?"

"Likely four or five of us might not have made it home tonight."

"That's it. He's usin' his head for something more than a place to hang a hat. Look at it. He's made a friend of Besovi and nobody is shot up."

Jed, soaking his battered hands, was not so sure. Besovi might have gone for a gun, or one of his hands might have. He had taken a long gamble and won; next time he might not be so lucky. At least, Rancho Casa Grande had one less enemy and one more friend.

If anything happened to him, Carol would need friends. Walt Seever was ominously quiet, and Jed was sure the man was waiting for proof that he was not Michael Latch. And that gave Jed an idea. It was a game at which two could play.

Carol was saddling her horse when he walked out in the morning. She glanced at him, her eyes hesitating on the bruise. "You seem to have a faculty for getting into trouble," she said, smiling.

He led out the black gelding. "I don't believe in ducking troubles. They just pile up on you. Sometimes they get too big to handle."

"You seem to have made a friend of Besovi."

"Why not? He's a good man, just used to taking in all he can put his hands on, but he'll prove a good neighbor." He hesitated, and then glanced off, afraid his eyes would give him away. "If anything happens to me, you'll need friends. I think Besovi would help you."

Her eyes softened. "Thank you, Mike." She hesitated just a little over the name. "You have already done much of what Uncle George just talked of doing."

Costa was gathering the herd Jed wanted to sell, and Pardo was riding with him. Jed did not ask Carol where she was going, but watched her ride away toward the valley. He threw a saddle on his own horse and cinched up. At the sound of horses' hoofs he turned.

Walt Seever was riding into the yard. With him were Harry Strykes and Gin Feeley. The fourth man was the one he had seen in the saloon who had told Walt he was not Michael Latch. Realizing he wore no guns, Jed felt naked and helpless. There was no one around the ranch house who he knew.

Seever drew rein and rested his hands on the pommel of his saddle. "Howdy! Howdy, Jed!"

No muscle changed on Jed Asbury's face. If trouble came, he was going right at Walt Seever.

"Smart play," Seever said, savoring his triumph. "If it hadn't been for me doubtin' you, you might have pulled it off."

Jed waited, watching.

"Now," Seever said, "your game is up. I suppose I should let you get on your horse an' ride, but we ain't about to."

"You mean to kill me like you did Latch and his friends?"

"Think you're smart, do you? Well, when you said that, you dug your own grave."

"I suppose your sour-faced friend here was one of those you sent to kill Latch," Jed commented. "He looks to be the kind."

"Let me kill him, Walt!" The man with the sour face had his hand on his gun. "Just let me kill him!"

Holding up a hand to stop the other man, Seever said: "What I want to know, is where you got them guns?"

"Out of the wagon, of course. The men you sent to stop Latch before he got here messed up. I'd just gotten away from a passel of Indians and was stark naked. I found clothes in the wagon. I also found the guns."

"About like I figured. Now we'll get rid of you, an' I'll have Casa Grande."

Jed was poised for a break, any kind of a break, and stalling for time. "Thieves like you always overlook important things. The men you sent messed up badly. They were in too much of a hurry and didn't burn the wagon. And what about Arden?"

"Arden? Who the devil is Arden?"

Jed had come a step nearer. They would get him, but he was going to kill Walt Seever. He chuckled. "They missed her, Walt. Arden is a girl. She was with Latch when he was killed."

"A girl?" Seever turned on the other man. "Clark, you never said anything about a girl."

"There wasn't any girl," Clark protested.

"He killed three of them, but she was out on the prairie to gather wild onions or something."

"That's a lie! There was only the three of them!" Clark shouted.

"What about those fancy clothes you threw around in the wagon? Think they were an old woman's clothes?"

Walt was furious. "Damn you, Clark. You said you got all of them."

"There wasn't no girl," Clark protested. "Anyway, I didn't see one."

"There was a girl, Walt, and she's safe. If

something goes wrong here, you will have to answer for it. You haven't a chance."

Seever's face was ugly with anger. "Anyway, we've got you. We've got you dead to rights." His hand moved toward his gun, but before Jed Asbury could move a muscle, there was a shot.

From behind Jed came Pat Flood's voice. "Keep your hands away from those guns, Walt. I can shoot the buttons off your shirt with this here rifle, and, in case that ain't enough, I got me a scatter-gun right beside me. Now you gents just unbuckle your belts, real easy now! You first, Seever!"

Jed dropped back swiftly and picked up the shotgun. The men shed their guns. "Now get off your hosses!" Flood ordered.

They dismounted.

Flood asked: "What you want done with 'em, boss? Should we bury them here or give them a runnin' chance?"

"Let them walk back to town," Jed suggested. "All but Clark. I want to talk to Clark."

Seever started to speak, but the buffalo gun and the shotgun were persuasive. He led the way.

"Let me go!" Clark begged. "They'll kill me!"

Jed gathered the gun belts and walked to the blacksmith shop, behind Clark.

"How much did you hear?" he asked Flood.

"All of it," the big blacksmith replied bluntly, "but my memory can be mighty poor. I judge a man by the way he handles himself, and you've been ridin' for the brand. I ain't interested in anything else."

Jed turned on Clark. "Get this straight. You've one chance to live, and you shouldn't have that. Tell us what happened, who sent you, and what you did." He glanced at Flood. "Take this down, every word."

"I got paper and pencil," Flood said. "I always keep a log."

"All right, Clark, a complete confession and you get your horse and a running start."

"Seever will kill me."

"Make your choice. You sign a confession or you can die right here at the end of a rope behind a runaway horse. Seever's not going to kill anybody, ever again."

Clark hesitated, and then he said: "I was broke in Ogden when Seever found me. I'd knowed him before. He told me I was to find this here wagon that was startin' West from Saint Louis. He said I was to make sure they never got here. I never knew there was a woman along."

"Who was with you?"

"Feller named Quinby and a friend of his'n named Buck Stanton. I met up with 'em in Laramie."

"Buck Stanton?"

At Jed's exclamation, Flood glanced at him: "You know them?"

"I killed Buck's brother Cal. They were crooked gamblers."

"Then you were the man they were huntin'!" Clark exclaimed.

"Where are they now?"

"Comin' this way, I suppose. Seever sent for 'em for some reason. Guess he figured they could come in here and prove you was somebody different than you said."

"Seever ordered the killing?"

"Yes, sir. He surely did."

A few more questions and the confession was signed. "Now get on that horse and get out of here before we change our minds and hang you."

"Do I get my guns?"

"You do not. Get going!"

Clark fairly threw himself into the saddle and left at a dead run.

Flood handed the confession to Jed. "Are you going to use it?"

"Not right now. I'll put it in the safe in the house. If Carol ever needs it, she can use it. If I brought it out now, it would prove that I am not Michael Latch."

"I knew you weren't him," Flood said. "Old George told me a good bit about him, but just seein' you around told me you'd covered a lot more country than he ever did."

"Does Carol know?"

"Don't reckon she does, but then she's a right canny lass."

If Stanton and Quinby were headed West, then

Seever must have telegraphed for them to come, and they would certainly ally themselves with Seever against him. As if he did not have trouble enough!

Costa and Jim Pardo rode into the yard, and Costa trotted his horse over to Jed, who was wearing the silver guns now.

"There were many cattle. More than expected. We came to see if the Willow Springs boys can help us."

"Later. Was Miss Carol out with you?"

"No, *señor*. She went to town."

Jed swore. "Flood, you take care of things here. We're riding into town."

Seever would stop at nothing now, and, if Quinby and Stanton had arrived in town, Jed's work would be cut out for him. No doubt Seever had known how to reach them, and it must have been from Stanton that Seever learned his name. A description from Seever would have been enough for Stanton to recognize who he was.

The town lay basking in a warm sun. In the distance the Sierras lifted snow-capped peaks against the blue sky. A man loitering in front of the Golden Strike stepped through the doors as Jed appeared in the street with his Casa Grande cowboys. Walt Seever stepped into the doorway, nonchalant, confident.

"Figured you'd be in. We sort of detained the lady, knowin' that would bring you. She can go loose now that you're where we want you."

Jed stepped down from the saddle. This was a trap, and they had ridden right into it.

"There's a gent in front of the express office, boss," Pardo said.

"Thanks, and watch the windows," Jed suggested. "Upstairs windows."

Jed was watching Seever. Trouble would begin with him. He moved away from his horse. No sense in getting a good animal killed. He did not look to see what Costa and Pardo were doing. They would be doing what was best for them and for what was coming.

"Glad you saved me the trouble of hunting you, Seever," he said.

Seever was on the edge of the boardwalk, a big man looking granite-hard and tough. "Save us both trouble. Folks here don't take to outsiders. They'd sooner have somebody like me runnin' the outfit than a stranger. Shuck your guns, get on your horse, and you can ride out of town."

"Don't do it, boss," Pardo warned. "He'll shoot you as soon as your back is turned."

"The ranch goes to Miss Carol, Seever. You might get me, but I promise you, you will die."

"Like hell!" Seever's hand swept for his gun. "I'll kill . . . !"

"Look out!" Pardo yelled.

Jed stepped aside as the rifle roared from the window over the livery barn, and his guns lifted. His first bullet took Walt Seever in the chest; his second went into the shadows behind a rifle muzzle in the barn loft.

Seever staggered into the street, his guns pounding lead into the street. Oblivious of the pounding guns around him, Jed centered his attention on Seever, and, when the man fell, the pistol dribbling from his fingers, Jed looked around, keeping his eyes from this man he had killed, hating the sight of what he had done.

Costa was down on one knee, blood staining the left sleeve of his shirt, but his face was expressionless, his pistol ready.

A dead man sprawled over the windowsill above the barn. A soft wind stirred his sandy hair. That would be Stanton. Pardo was holstering his gun. There was no sign of Strykes or Feeley.

"You all right, boss?" Pardo asked.

"All right. How about you?"

Tony Costa was getting to his feet. "Caught one in the shoulder," he said. "It's not bad."

Heads were appearing in doors and windows, but nobody showed any desire to come outside. Then a door slammed down the street, and Carol was running to them.

"Are you hurt?" She caught his arm. "Were you shot?"

He slid an arm around her as she came up to him, and it was so natural that neither of them noticed. "Better get that shoulder fixed up, Costa." He glanced down at Carol. "Where did they have you?"

"Strykes and Feeley were holding me in a house across the street. When Feeley saw you were not alone, he wanted Harry Strykes to leave. Feeley looked out the door and Pat Flood saw him."

"Flood?"

"He followed you in, knowing there'd be trouble. He came in behind them and had me take their guns. He was just going out to help you when the shooting started."

"Carol. . . ." He hesitated. "I've got a confession to make. I am not Michael Latch."

"Oh? Is that all? I've known that all the time. You see, I was Michael Latch's wife."

"His what?"

"Before I married him, I was Carol Arden James. He was the only one who ever called me Arden. During the time we were coming West, I was quite ill, so I stayed in the wagon and Clark never saw me at all.

"He convinced Michael there was a wagon train going by way of Santa Fe that would take us through sooner, and, if we could catch them, it would help. It was all a lie to get us away from the rest of the wagons, but Michael listened, as the train we were with was going only as far as Laramie. After we were on the trail, Clark left us to locate the wagon train, as he said. Randy Kenner and Mike decided to camp, and I went over the hill to a small pool to bathe. When I was dressing, I heard shooting, and, believing it was

Indians, I crept to the top of a hill so I could see our wagon.

"It was all over. Clark had ridden up with two men and opened fire at once. They'd had no warning, no chance. Randy was not dead when I saw them. One of the men kicked a gun out of his hand . . . he was already wounded . . . and shot him again. There was nothing I could do, so I simply hid."

"But how did you get here?"

"When they left, I did not go back to the wagon. I simply couldn't, and I was afraid they might return. So I started walking back to the wagon train we had left. I hadn't gone far when I found Old Nellie, our saddle mare. She knew me and came right up to me, so I rode her back to the wagon train. I came from Laramie by stage."

"Then you knew all the time that I was faking?"

"Yes, but when you stopped Walt, I whispered to Costa not to say anything."

"He knew as well?"

"Yes. I'd showed him my marriage license, which I always carried with me, along with a little money."

"Why didn't you say something? I was having a battle with my conscience, trying to decide what was right, always knowing I'd have to explain sooner or later."

"You were doing much better with the ranch than Michael could have. Michael and I grew up together and were much more like brother and sister than husband and wife. When he heard from his Uncle George, we were married, and we liked each other."

Suddenly it dawned on Jed that they were standing in the middle of the street and he had his arm around Carol. Hastily he withdrew it.

"Why didn't you just claim the estate as Michael's wife?"

"Costa was afraid Seever would kill me. We had not decided what to do when you appeared."

"What about these guns?"

"My father made them. He was a gunsmith and he had made guns for Uncle George. These were a present to Mike when he started West."

His eyes avoided hers. "Carol, I'll get my gear and move on. The ranch is yours, and with Seever gone you will be all right."

"I don't want you to go."

He thought his ears deceived him. "You . . . what?"

"Don't go, Jed. Stay with us. I can't manage the ranch alone, and Costa has been happy since you've been here. We need you, Jed. I . . . I need you."

"Well," he spoke hesitantly, "there are things to be done and cattle to be sold, and that quarter section near Willow Springs could be irrigated."

Pardo, watching, glanced at Flood. "I think he's going to stay, Pat."

"Sure," Flood said. "Ships an' women, they all need a handy man around the place."

Carol caught Jed's sleeve. "Then you'll stay?"

He smiled. "What would Costa do without me?"

Acknowledgments

"The Lion Hunter and the Lady" under the byline Jim Mayo first appeared in *Giant Western* (8/51). Copyright © 1951 by Best Publications, Inc. Copyright not renewed.

"The Trail to Peach Meadow Cañon" under the byline Jim Mayo first appeared in *Giant Western* (10/49). Copyright © 1952 by Best Publications, Inc. Copyright not renewed.

"Riding for the Brand" under the byline Jim Mayo first appeared in *Thrilling Western* (9/48). Copyright © 1948 by Standard Magazines, Inc. Copyright not renewed.

Center Point Publishing
600 Brooks Road ● PO Box 1
Thorndike ME 04986-0001 USA

(207) 568-3717

US & Canada:
1 800 929-9108
www.centerpointlargeprint.com